PRAISE FOR KANA WU

"You know when you go to a movie and watch a lighthearted rom-com? The closing credits are rolling over, and a young singer songwriter's theme song is being played in a movie theater. When you walk out of the theater, you are greeted by a warm rainy city and gentle summer breeze. That was how I felt like when I finished this new lighthearted romance. This book has a very positive vibe to it." — Goodreads Reviewer, 4 stars, on *A Warm Rainy Day In Tokyo*.

"...Highly recommended for readers who are tired of the typical chick lit romance, and are ready for something light as air and just as refreshing." — K.C. Finn for Readers' Favorite, 5 stars, on *No Romance Allowed*.

"An agreeably warm story that bounces along effortlessly on the genuine chemistry of its lead characters, Rory and Peter, Wu takes the much-loved tropes of the genre and makes them her own." — The BookViral Review, on *No Romance Allowed*.

"Readers who enjoy romance novels with a touch of suspense will appreciate this book." — OnlineBookClub.org, 4 stars, on *No Romance Allowed*.

"Wu offers a relatable tale of a couple struggling to adapt to a long-distance relationship. Peppered with intriguing dynamics of co-workers who threaten fidelity, and judgmental family members sowing doubt, there is palpable tension sustained throughout this compact novel. The main characters are loveable and endearing, and Wu's handling of past regrets and secrets withheld endow the couple with a blithe honesty and vulnerability that is sure to warm the hearts of readers of this engaging series." — Self-Publishing Review, 4 stars, on *No Secrets Allowed*

"There wasn't any toxic character trying to take the other down. It was pure love and we all need that nowadays." — Goodreads Reviewer, 4 stars, on *A Warm Rainy Day In Tokyo*.

"A Warm Rainy Day in Tokyo not only offers a Hallmark style love story, but also an intriguing peek into life in Japan through the eyes of a foreigner. Kana Wu's characters are lovable and easy to root for, and she builds a masterful and immersive setting for them as well." —Goodreads Reviewer, 4 stars, on *A Warm Rainy Day In Tokyo*.

"The plot of this book surprised me and kept me interested." — Goodreads Reviewer, 5 stars, on *A Warm Rainy Day In Tokyo*.

"I enjoyed this book even more than the first one. It had a bit of twist and turn with wonderful characters. It was a fantastic one-sitting read for me. Nothing is better than sitting with a book that pulls you out of the real world." — Goodreads Reviewer, 5 stars, on *No Secrets Allowed*.

"Verdict: It's good!" — Goodreads Reviewer, 4 stars, on *No Romance Allowed*.

OTHER NOVELS BY KANA WU

No Romance Allowed

No Secrets Allowed

A Warm Rainy Day In Tokyo

Dear Danielle Urban,
Enjoy the read.
Kana Wu
08/14 2023

She Calls Her Mom

Copyright © 2023 by Kana Wu

For more about this author, please visit https://www.kanawuauthor.com/

Interior and Cover Design by Asya Blue Design

eBook ISBN: 978-1-7357676-7-3
paperback ISBN: 978-1-7357676-6-6
Main category—FIC044000 FICTION / Women
Other category—FIC045020 FICTION / Family Life / General

First Edition

an emotional page turner with an unexpected twist

SHE CALLS HER MOM

a novella

KANA WU

*To all young moms out there who navigate the
challenges of motherhood on their own,
this story is for you.*

TABLE OF CONTENTS

CHAPTER 1

With her hands over her ears, Zoey Matthew squeezed her eyes shut and imagined she was standing in a garden, surrounded by fragrant flowers, colorful butterflies, and chirping birds. The wailing from the corner of the bedroom grew louder and louder, seeping through her orange earplugs.

Next to the king-size bed, four-month-old Ella Dawson was shrieking in her crib. Her tiny fingers clenched, her feet kicked in the air, and her face was red. She looked ready to explode.

Zoey loved the baby to pieces, and wherever they went, people praised Ella's angelic face, blue eyes, and curly blonde hair. They had no idea that little bundle of joy had the deafening scream of a banshee.

If God had remembered to make an off switch for babies, being a mom would have been much easier.

Leaning back against the window frame, Zoey massaged her temples. In desperation, she pulled at her brown hair, which was tied in a loose ponytail, until it hung in messy, wild strands around her face. She'd bounced, fed, and bathed Ella, then changed her. She'd checked to make sure the plastic fastener wasn't sticking out and run her fingers across the diaper to make sure it felt smooth before putting it on the baby. Zoey had sung until her throat hurt, but the pitch of Ella's wail kept rising. Right now, leaving her alone on the bed seemed like the best option.

Exhaling, Zoey turned to gaze out the window of the master bedroom. Her sister had bought this townhouse with her fiancé, Richard Dawson, two-and-half years ago before they were married. Zoey admired her sister's choice to pay a high monthly mortgage in exchange for this incredible view.

She peered out into the green canyon and could make out the majestic Saddleback Mountains in the distance. The afternoon sunlight shone through the thick rain clouds as if the rays were attempting to push them away. It had been pouring nonstop for the past two days. After the first ten hours, a flash-flood warning had been sent out, and once the rain subsided, the local news broadcast footage of mudslides that had struck two coastal towns in Orange County.

In the room, the tiny baby had already flooded her polka-dot tunic with tears. Feeling hopeless, heat swelled behind Zoey's eyes as she wished everything would return to the way it had been before, in her old life as a billing accountant.

She almost missed the bitchy payroll manager who never looked her in the eye when they bumped into each other in the hallway and the jealous tattletale coworker who seemed ready to broadcast her pointless mistakes. They seemed mellow compared to this tantrum-throwing baby.

Life was unfair.

Zoey would never forget the moment when police had knocked on the door of her apartment forty-five days earlier. It was seven in the morning, and she'd just finished her breakfast. Her stomach churned, and she almost threw up as the officer told her about the hit-and-run that had taken Katya and Richard Dawson's lives. They'd been on California SR-14, on their way to Mammoth Lakes for their first trip as a family, when the driver lost control of the stolen F-150. Ella had survived because Katya shielded her with her body.

When the police brought Zoey to the morgue to identify the bodies, the bruises and wounds on her sister's face and neck had been stitched up and cleaned. Her knees trembled when she received the bag of their personal belongings gathered from the debris. Zoey bawled her eyes out for days, although she knew that wouldn't bring them back to life.

Katya had been more than a sister to Zoey. Zoey was seven and Katya was fifteen when their dad died from an overdose and their mom ran away without a word to them two weeks after that. Their maternal grandma, Evie, had taken them in. When she passed away four years later, she left the house to them. The sisters lived there for another year before they decided to sell it and use the money to pay for their education.

Zoey couldn't recall her mom's face because Katya had burned all their family pictures and memorabilia in anger. Never had it crossed her mind that her gentle and thoughtful sister could be so violent. Her face was distorted in rage as she threw a burning stick upon the piles, watched the fire swallow them up, and threw the ashes into a garbage can. Zoey never mentioned her mom in front of her sister because she was afraid it would ignite Katya's rage all over again. Still, she remembered their mom had beautiful blonde hair and blue eyes, like Ella. But other than that, Zoey didn't have any memories of her. Perhaps she'd buried them deep in her mind.

The thing she regretted most was that she hadn't answered the phone the morning Katya left for that deathly trip. Zoey had already been late for work and ignored her sister's call. Now, she'd never know what Katya wanted to say.

Once the news of the couple's death was announced, people—mostly friends of Katya and Richard and some close neighbors—began rotating in and out of the townhouse, giving Zoey their condolences. She didn't know them, but it didn't matter because every day was a blur.

After the cremation and memorial service, Harold Young from Young Law Firm, LLC, invited Zoey to his office and introduced himself as the executor and attorney for the Dawson living trust. The sixty-year-old man read the will, which stated that Ella was her parents' sole beneficiary. All their assets would be given to her when she was twenty-five years old. In the event that Ella was underage when they died, her guardian would manage all the liquid assets until she reached that age. Katya had chosen Zoey as Ella's guardian.

Speechless, Zoey had frozen in her seat. She was barely twenty-one, and her career had just begun. How could she be a mom to an infant? What about the dreams she wanted to pursue? Should she sacrifice them all? What about her love life? Was there any man who could possibly be interested in her—a woman with a baby—even though the baby wasn't hers?

She was haunted by these thoughts and, after leaving the attorney's office, drove four hundred miles north instead of going home. She ignored the congested traffic when entering downtown Los Angeles and navigated the orange barrels around the highway work zone on autopilot. Gorgeous beach scenes and the tunnels of Pacific Coast Highway always caught her eye when she would drive through there, but not this time. Her mind focused on only one thing: driving as far as possible from home.

Near Monterey, she stopped at Lover's Point and stayed in a budget hotel for several nights. She switched her phone off because she didn't want anyone to reach her.

On her fourth day there, Nora Oh—her best friend since elementary school—found her sitting alone on the sand by the seashore, watching the ebb and flow of the waves. Zoey's ex-boyfriend, Terrance Jensen, also known as Tian Jie—his Chinese given name—or TJ, had brought her, then waited patiently a little off to the side for Nora to go talk to her.

Zoey shouldn't have been surprised TJ had figured out where she was. He'd taken her to explore Monterey the day after her graduation, and they'd found Lover's Point. Zoey had fallen in love with the place instantly and begged TJ to take her back there. Alas, their relationship had ended. Zoey decided to leave TJ and began dating her coworker, who she thought was more mature. In the end, that courtship was as short as a burning candle.

"Why are you out here without telling anyone? Is it because of what the attorney said?" Nora asked, her voice soft as she sat down next to her on the warm sand, studying Zoey's troubled face. Normally, Zoey would have made a comment because, for once, her best friend didn't seem concerned about having beach sand stuck on her feet and short pants. "What did he tell you?"

"Katya wants me to be Ella's guardian because I'm her only kin. My grandparents passed away years ago. Both my parents are only children. My first cousins live outside California. Richard's adoptive parents live in Sydney, and they're already eighty." Zoey looked at Nora, then beyond, to TJ sitting on the sand with his back against a big rock just a few feet away.

She continued, the desperation in her voice growing. "If Ella were older, taking care of her would be easy. But she's a baby and won't understand what I say, just as I don't understand her. I don't even know how to change a diaper. How can I raise her? I love Ella, but I can't be her mom."

"But running away isn't the answer." Nora touched her arm. "I know you're upset and everything seems hopeless, but do you feel peaceful right now?"

Zoey choked back her tears and lowered her head, considering her friend's question.

"Is there another option if you don't want to be Ella's guardian?" TJ asked after a moment's silence.

"Yes, giving up my right of custody to the state. If I do that, Harold will find a good family to raise her. I can even help him interview them, so I'll know what kind of people they are," Zoey whispered.

"I think that's a good idea, right? Lots of people aren't able to have kids of their own. Ella is a sweet baby, and someone will happily take her," Nora said.

"But I can't abandon her." Zoey shook her head adamantly. "I can't imagine Ella living in a stranger's home." She covered her face, sobbing.

Nora and TJ exchanged brief glances. They sat in silence, watching the waves crash against the shore as they waited for her to calm down.

She sniffed and wiped her forehead with the back of her hand. "Katya must be mad at me. When my dad passed away and my mom left us, she stayed and raised me with Granny, but now that Ella needs me, I'm washing my hands of her."

"You're just scared." Nora looked at her with sympathy. "If I were you, I'd be kicking, screaming, and throwing stuff."

Zoey pushed her feet deeper into the sand. She wished she could do those things, but naturally, she wasn't as explosive as Nora.

"Why don't we go home, Zoey?" TJ suggested. "Once you calm down, you can make a decision. No matter what you choose, you won't be alone. Nora and I have been your friends for years, so you can come to us whenever you need, including when you need a babysitter."

Nora nodded. "He's right. Let's go home. But right now, the most important thing is getting changed. You must've worn the same clothes for days." She put a bag in front of Zoey, wrinkling her nose.

Zoey took the bag and returned to her hotel to take a quick shower and change into the blue jeans and navy-blue T-shirt Nora had packed for her. Then she went back home with TJ and Nora.

Three days later, she drove to Harold's office to meet with the attorney again and tell him about her decision to become Ella's guardian. Tension built in her stomach as she caught sight of the five-story black glass building with red trim, and her hand trembled as she turned off the car engine.

Did she make the right decision?

Harold's fatherly tone calmed her down as she sat in front of him in his office. "Every choice comes with a consequence," he said. "To those who don't know your story, you will be Ella's mom, a young and unmarried woman. Although there are many more young, single moms now than a few decades ago, you should be aware that being a single mom isn't an easy life. And some men won't date a woman with a baby."

Zoey was aware of these downsides, especially the last one. She figured it would be better for her not to think seriously about romance until Ella turned eighteen.

Harold arranged the paperwork and suggested Zoey move out of the apartment she shared with Nora and into Katya's house. It had everything she needed to take care of Ella. Zoey would have preferred to have the baby come stay with her, as her sister's house was a forty-five-minute commute away from her office, while the drive from the apartment only took ten minutes. After a brief debate with Harold, however, Zoey gave up and agreed to move.

Harold didn't just brush Zoey and Ella off after he'd executed his job. He gave Zoey a list of support groups for young moms, where she could learn from these women's experiences. He also arranged for Lena—the babysitter Katya had used—to help with Ella whenever she needed.

For two weeks, Lena taught Zoey about essential infant care, including how to make homemade baby food. She was a kind and patient instructor and didn't mind repeating herself. Although she did cover her eyes with a hand and murmur, "*Ay, Dios mío,*" when Zoey put on rubber gloves before changing Ella's diaper, or held Ella over her head after feeding one morning and she threw up all over her, or when she became frustrated over installing a car seat in a convertible stroller.

Nora also kept her promise to help whenever she was available. Sometimes, she and her boyfriend, Jared, came over to watch Ella when Zoey had to work overtime. Zoey didn't want to ask for TJ's assistance. She had her pride.

Aside from learning to care for an infant, Zoey had to deal with Rocket, Katya's precious Shiba Inu. That dog was spoiled and knew he was handsome because whenever Katya took him out for a walk, people would say things like, "what a handsome Shiba Inu," or "He looks like that dog in the movie *Hachiko*." And Rocket would strut with his chest puffed out and little nose up in the air, enjoying the praises.

Zoey didn't like him and wished he had never existed. Rocket, for his part, didn't like her either since she always shooed him away like a pest.

Juggling her time between work and a baby was already challenging, and now she had to find time to walk Rocket twice a day for thirty to forty minutes each time. Hiring a dog walker would be expensive, but luckily, Lena didn't mind walking him in the evening before she left for the day.

For a while, everything seemed smooth, but it didn't last long. The odds were against Zoey.

Nora's parents asked her to work at their convenience store after two employees were caught stealing money from the store's cash register, so she didn't have time to help out anymore. Around the same time, Lena's husband had a severe stroke and was paralyzed from the waist down, so she had to quit to take care of him.

Clementine, Lena's replacement, wasn't as good as her predecessor. Although she received the same pay, she wasn't willing to clean the house or come over in the evenings when Zoey had to work overtime. She only wanted to take care of Ella, period. She ignored Rocket and often didn't feed him or replace his water. Zoey had to buy him automatic food and water dispensers. As much as she wanted to fire the woman, Clementine was the best nanny she could afford.

Attempting to weather the storm, Zoey sacrificed her sleep to manage the household. Just twelve days into her new life without Lena and Nora, she surrendered and handed in her resignation letter. The stress at work and at home was making her lose weight and just wasn't going to work long term.

Tears rolled down her cheeks as she drove from the office parking lot on her last day. While the utility company hadn't been an ideal work environment, she had been proud of her job there, as only a few people in her graduating class had been hired immediately upon graduating.

The doorbell rang downstairs, interrupting her reverie and pulling her back to the present.

"Who's that?" she muttered to herself as she glanced at her smartwatch—3:40 on Wednesday afternoon. Maybe an Amazon delivery driver brought another mysterious package?

Since last month, Zoey had been receiving weekly deliveries from Amazon Fresh containing an array of groceries from frozen food to fresh fruits. She asked around, but no one admitted to sending them. She considered refusing the bags but, in the end, decided to accept them.

Coming down the stairs, Zoey removed her earplugs and then opened the door. She was struck by an earthy smell of rain as the door flew open, revealing a man of average height wearing a dark suit. He was standing on the doorstep with a bouquet of white lilies tucked under his left arm and an umbrella under his right.

"Are you Zoey, Katya Dawson's sister?" he asked hesitantly.

"Yes. Who are you?" She studied him.

The man was young and good-looking, maybe in his midtwenties. His fair skin made his black eyes pop under their thick eyebrows, and his dark brown hair was cropped short. It wouldn't surprise her if the man was one of her sister's friends. Unlike Zoey, Katya had been a social butterfly. Although it had almost been one-and-a-half months since she'd passed away, people continued coming to give their condolences. Some brought fruit, flowers, toys, or clothes for Ella.

The man was just about to open his mouth when Ella began her banshee scream again.

Zoey rubbed her forehead, then glanced at the man, who was now frowning and gazing up toward the second floor.

"Is that Ella? Why is she crying like that?" His concern was written all over his face.

"How do you know my niece's name?" Zoey felt alarmed.

"I'm Derek Waltz. I've known your sister and Richard for years. I'm Mr. Young's paralegal." The man took a business card from his pocket and handed it to her. "I wanted to give my condolences in person, but I've been out of town on business." Derek handed her the bouquet. "I'm so sorry for your loss."

"Thank you." As Zoey took the flowers, Ella's scream grew louder. "Sorry, I don't mean to be rude, but I have to check on her." She stepped back to close the door.

"I know we just met, but may I see Ella? Maybe I can help," Derek said.

Zoey looked at him, considering his offer before shaking her head. "Thank you, but I doubt you can help because I've already tried everything. I've bathed her, fed her, and changed her diaper, but she won't stop. The sitter might know how to calm her, and she will be here in"—she looked at her watch—"thirty min—"

The wailing continued.

"Listen. You look tired. Let me try," Derek said. "If it doesn't work, as you'd said, the sitter will be here soon anyway. If you're worried about my intentions, leave the door open so people can see me."

Zoey's lips twitched. She didn't know him, but he was Katya's friend. After a brief deliberation, she nodded. "Okay. Come on in." She opened the door and pointed to the kitchen. "Please wash your hands there first, and then you can wait on the sofa while I bring Ella down." Dropping the business card on the coffee table, she rushed up the stairs.

Ella was still screaming as Zoey brought her down. She was furious and wriggling hard in her aunt's arms. The baby's little foot made contact with Derek's chin when Zoey handed her over.

"Sorry...sorry," she stammered.

"That's okay." Derek's voice was comforting. He seemed like a natural holding Ella. "Shhhhh...Don't cry, Ella...shhhhhh...don't cry, sweet baby...don't cry, little one...." He bounced Ella gently and began to hum.

Initially, Zoey didn't recognize the song, but she soon realized it was "Baby Mine" from the old Disney movie *Dumbo*. Her mom used to sing it to her when she was a child. Mixed emotions flooded her as the song brought back the sweet memory, and for the first time in years, a feeling of longing for her mom emerged. Zoey blinked hard and concentrated on Derek and Ella.

Derek sang the song three times, and Ella's whimpering gradually stopped. Maybe his voice had soothed her, or the baby was simply tired from crying.

"She's already sleeping," he whispered. Zoey looked down at her niece, who was snoozing soundly, tears still in her eyes.

"Thank God. I thought she'd never stop," she whispered, holding her hand out for the baby.

"Ready?" Derek asked in a softer voice.

Zoey nodded. Their arms brushed as he transferred Ella back to her. "I'll take her up," she said.

"And I'd better go now." Derek walked to the door but turned around and wrote something on the business card on the table.

"Are you sure you don't want some water?" Zoey asked.

"That's okay. I'm fine." He turned to her. "By the way, I wrote down my number in case you ever need my help."

He smiled when Zoey mouthed "thank you" before closing the door behind him. For a few seconds, she stared at the door. Was he an angel in human form? Or a male version of Mary Poppins, the way he'd popped up in the middle of her chaotic day and calmed Ella?

Exhaling, she spun around and climbed the stairs, careful not to wake the baby.

CHAPTER 2

It was a sunny Thursday afternoon, but Zoey wasn't paying much attention to the weather. She bit her inner cheek because the police seemed to be getting nowhere on the hit-and-run case.

The only lead they had was a set of pictures from the roadside cameras on the freeway. They were blurry stills of the driver getting out of the truck, crouching near a back window of her sister's Lexus, then getting in the truck again and driving off. It had been foggy that night, and it was hard to determine the person's face or gender. The only thing the police could say for certain was that they had shoulder-length brown hair.

Zoey massaged her temples, easing her throbbing head as she tried to reconcile Katya's bank statements with the overdue bills scattered on the floor next to her. Earlier, she'd called the companies and explained the situation and was relieved when they all agreed to waive the late fees.

Sitting on the carpet with her back against the couch, Zoey frowned, looking at the total in the expense column in the spreadsheet she'd created.

"What did they do?" she muttered under her breath. She threw the statement down beside her on the right and opened another envelope from the pile on her left. Three feet away, the tip of a furry ear flicked each time she let a paper fall. Rocket watched her with one of his big brown eyes, then closed it again a second later. Next to him, Ella was sleeping in her swing with a pacifier in her mouth, snoring softly.

Zoey rubbed her tired hazel-brown eyes, unsettled by her sister's spending, and wondered how the couple had managed to keep up this lifestyle on their monthly incomes. For example, this mortgage cost them $2,700. They were paying off two cars for a total of $1,200 a month—a BMW M3, which belonged to Richard, and a Lexus, which belonged to Katya. The Lexus was now totaled because of the accident.

There were also two credit cards with a total balance of $7,300. In total, they were paying more than $11,000 a month. That was crazy!

Living in Orange County was expensive, but Katya and Richard had had lucrative incomes as a marketing manager and a senior programmer. If he and her sister had lived thriftily, the amount in their three bank accounts could be more than fifty thousand dollars. Good thing they hadn't forgotten to open a college fund for Ella when she was born.

Zoey tapped her fingers on the table, trying to figure out how to increase her savings. The two jet skis—she was sure her sister and Richard had never used them—would be gone this week, sold for fifteen grand through ads on the Nextdoor app.

The BMW was two years old and in excellent condition. Zoey could quickly get around fifty grand for that. She wasn't into the sporty car, so selling it was better than letting it sit in the garage, collecting dust. Her four-year-old Honda Civic was big enough to shuttle her, Ella, and Rocket from one place to another. It had already been paid off and was well-maintained.

Zoey wrote down Nora's name next to the BMW on her list. Nora's uncle worked at an auto dealership and might be able to help her sell it at a reasonable price. She didn't want to call her now, as she figured Nora might be busy helping at her parents' convenience store, Oh Mart, where they had a "no cellphone" policy for employees.

She was in the process of writing TJ's name next to Nora's when her pen stopped midair. His family owned an auto dealership and had a certified pre-owned program that might be more beneficial for her. Too bad. Not interested in asking for his help, she crossed out his name.

At that moment, something rough and wet touched her elbow. Rocket looked up at her, wagging his tail. A soft bubbling noise coming from the swing indicated Ella had woken up too.

"Do you want to walk?" Zoey asked the two-year-old tan dog.

He woofed and took a few steps toward the door, then turned back.

"Okay, let's walk with Ella after I feed her."

Rocket loved Ella, and he barked at the sound of her name.

Zoey smiled at the dog, amazed they had become friends because they initially hadn't liked each other. The horrible accident had forced them to learn how to get along well, and ultimately, she found he wasn't as bad as she'd thought. He always walked on her left side and never pulled his leash to chase rabbits or squirrels. He also waited patiently whenever Zoey transferred Ella from the car seat to the stroller and didn't react when other dogs passed.

Once they were in the front yard, Zoey put the leash on him and tied it to the stroller handle. The storage space at the bottom of the stroller was filled with a diaper bag, a checkered blanket, bottled water, Rocket's bowl, Ella's foldable bed, Zoey's Kindle, and snacks for the three. Ella was lying on her back watching her aunt with her blue eyes, babbling and giggling. Zoey smiled and softly tapped the tip of the baby's nose with her finger.

The housing complex was quiet at that hour—no cars parked at the curb or in the carports. Most people were at work or doing errands.

Zoey pushed the stroller to a community park called Green Wood. It was farther from her house—about a thirty-minute walk—but better than the two small parks nearby. Green Wood had a huge field that could be used for football or soccer, an expansive grass area, a structured picnic area, a playground, and a rose garden for strolling.

Tall pine trees offered some shade as they walked. When they arrived, the playground was packed with children. The older kids were on the climbers or slides, while the little kids were digging in the sandbox or playing on the spring riders. Their moms and sitters were watching them from the sidelines.

Zoey continued on to the grassy area. Mingling with the parents at the playground gave her a headache. Once they learned she was a new mom, they tended to lecture her—they meant well, but were too helpful. Besides, Zoey was tired of explaining how she'd ended up caring for her niece. Repeating the story was like rubbing salt in her raw wound.

Near the rose garden entrance, she found a perfect spot on higher ground, with bushy trees towering above and tall scrubs that worked as a natural noise barrier, blocking out the voices from the playground. Zoey spread the blanket out on the ground, and they settled in. From her foldable bed, Ella gazed up at the sky as if she was counting the clouds. Rocket stood in front of them, his leash tied around a corkscrew-shaped stake. He lifted his nose, maybe sniffing the fresh air or trying to detect the scent of nearby squirrels or rabbits.

There was no one in the grassy area but them. Zoey loved listening to the sounds of the light afternoon breeze rustling the leaves, and the baby and Rocket seemed to be enjoying it too. Ella's eyes fluttered before she fell asleep. The dog sniffed at her blanket and let out a wide yawn, then lay down by Zoey's feet.

She opened her Kindle cover and began reading her book. Occasionally, she tore her eyes away from her reading to check on Rocket and Ella. Something expanded in her chest when she saw them sleeping so peacefully.

Thirty minutes passed. Ella woke up and started fussing. Zoey took her bottle from an insulated bag and put it in her mouth, and she sucked her milk hungrily. She gazed at her aunt, occasionally cooing.

"Aww, look at the baby," a voice remarked.

Startled, Zoey looked up to find a woman standing close by. She couldn't make out the stranger's face, as she was backlit by the afternoon sun. However, people in this commuter town were friendlier than in the city she used to live in and bumping into neighbors in a church, a hospital, a grocery store, or a movie theater was normal, so she wasn't too surprised.

"Hello," Zoey said.

"Hi." The woman smiled and lowered herself to the ground where Zoey could see her clearly. She had light, wavy brown hair with some gray mixed in, which stuck out of her ivory-colored hat. There was a tiny black mole on the corner of her lower lip. Pushing her sunglasses up on her head, she revealed her amber eyes. The laugh lines around them were profound. She must have been in her midfifties.

"How old is she?" The woman gazed at Ella with adoration in her eyes.

"Four months."

"And you must be her handsome bodyguard." She turned to Rocket, who was watching her cautiously. He didn't growl or bark, but the hair on his neck was standing straight up.

Ella stopped drinking and pushed the bottle away from her mouth. She watched the woman, seeming to understand the conversation, then waved her hand near Rocket. He automatically licked her little fingers with his wet tongue.

Zoey chuckled. "Yes, Rocket has loved Ella since she was born and is always protective of her."

"His name is Rocket?" There was a hint of amusement in the woman's voice.

Zoey grinned. That was a common reaction when people heard the dog's name. "Yes. It was taken from Rocket Raccoon from the Guardians of the Galaxy series." She purposely omitted the fact that her sister was the one who had chosen it.

"I don't follow movies nowadays, but they're so cute together," the stranger said, turning to Zoey. "Do you mind if I sit here for a moment? I sprained my ankle a couple weeks ago, and it still gets stiff if I walk too long."

"Sure." Zoey took a container of snacks and put it in her backpack to clear some space.

"Thanks." Grunting, the woman used her hand to support her body as she sat down on the blanket. She crossed her right leg over her left knee and gave it a light massage. "I'm Claudia Erickson, by the way, and I live in a Kensington apartment on Acacia Street. A bit far from here, but I like walking in this park." She smiled.

Zoey always passed that building when she went to work. "I'm Zoey Matthew, and this is Ella and Rocket. We live in the townhouse complex between Olympiad and Marguerite." She pointed west. "Nice to meet you, Claudia."

"Nice to meet you, Zoey, Ella, and Rocket." Again, the woman grinned at the baby and the dog.

Upon hearing her name, Ella turned to Claudia and giggled, a mix of saliva and milk pooling around the sides of her mouth.

"Ella has a sweet smile. I could watch it for hours," Claudia commented, turning to Zoey. "Are you new to the area? I usually recognize moms who come here regularly, but not you."

"Yes, I moved here one-and-a-half months ago. Usually, I go to the parks in my neighborhood. This is my first time coming here," Zoey answered.

"I see. No wonder I haven't seen you and your pack before." She held out two treats from her pocket. "Is it okay if I give Rocket a couple of milk bones?"

"Sure." Zoey nodded and watched the woman place the snacks near Rocket's front paw.

The Shiba looked at Zoey as if asking for approval and sniffed, gobbling it up once she nodded.

"I love dogs but can't have one in my apartment, so I always carry these in my pocket for ones I bump into here," Claudia said, looking pleased as Rocket licked crumbs from around his mouth.

"Yes, my old apartment had the same policy, but some tenants ignored it. When the management found out, they had to pay a high fine," said Zoey. "Good thing my sister's HOA allows home-owners to have pets. Just two, though."

"Oh, Rocket is your sister's dog?" the woman asked, letting him sniff the pocket where she kept the milk bones.

"Yes. But now I take care of him," Zoey answered as shortly as possible, then turned to Ella. "Are you already full?"

Claudia didn't press, just gave them a thoughtful gaze as Zoey put the bottle back into the insulated bag. She smiled at Ella and played peek-a-boo with her for a few minutes before saying, "I wish I could stay longer and talk to you, but I must go." She pushed herself up with her hands to stand up. "I hope to see you guys next time."

"Yes, I hope to see you again, Claudia," Zoey said. She was starting to like the woman. She wasn't intrusive and hadn't asked any more questions. "This spot is perfect for us, so if we're around, you'll find us here."

"Okay, that's easy." Claudia waved and sauntered toward the exit with her hands clasped behind her. Her light white jacket flapped as she crossed the empty parking lot.

Zoey tried to read again, but the words seemed to swarm, and after just a few minutes, she gave up and closed the device. She took Rocket's ball thrower and played with him for a while before leaving the park.

CHAPTER 3

Rocket had been a six-month-old puppy with a big head and a tiny body when Katya brought him home. The shelter had raided the puppy mill where he was born and confiscated him along with the other puppies and their moms, taking them to a safe facility where they could be cared for until they were ready to be adopted.

The Shiba had adored Katya and trailed after her like a second shadow. Richard always teased her, saying, "If you were lost, we'd find you by following Rocket."

A year later, when Katya was six months pregnant, the dog had leaned his head on her stomach as if he knew his future human sister was inside. Once Ella was born, he always slept near her crib.

As far as Zoey remembered, Rocket had never been sick—until now. She found a pool of vomit next to his bed downstairs, and the Shiba had curled up and ignored her. As she looked closer, she saw the vomit was dark red. Her stomach dropped. Could the snack Claudia gave him yesterday have caused this? That wasn't possible because it had been the same brand he usually ate.

He didn't wag his tail or sniff the piece of unsalted chicken Zoey had cooked for him on the grill. Besides Ella, Rocket was one of the most important links she had to her sister. When Zoey was missing Katya, he seemed to feel it and would show off the skills his previous owner had taught him: crawling, upside-down bicycling, rolling, and standing up. His tongue hung out as he watched Zoey smiling at him. He had also been a loyal companion and would leave Ella to sleep on Zoey's slippers when she watched TV or read on the sofa.

Pain stabbed her stomach as she looked at his lethargic body. "Please be healthy again, Rocket. Ella needs you. I need you too," she whispered, caressing him.

Rocket lifted his head a few inches to lick her fingers with his tongue, which felt warmer than usual.

Worrying about his condition, Zoey called his regular vet and was happy when the office agreed to see him within an hour. Then she called Clementine to take care of Ella while she was gone and felt her blood boil as she heard the unwillingness in the babysitter's voice to come to work earlier than usual. If she'd had another option, she'd have fired her on the spot.

Traffic to the vet was light, but the veterinary hospital parking lot was packed at ten in the morning. Zoey parked her car carefully in the last free spot next to a silver hatchback at the very end.

Her heart pounded when she got out and saw a white Prius with a blue vet tech decal affixed to the rear window. She remembered TJ's beaming face when he'd stuck it there once he got the job in the hospital. After she broke up with him, she'd begged Katya to find a new vet for Rocket, but she wouldn't listen.

"The vets in the hospital aren't money-oriented, and they always provide better service for less, unlike the place near us," she'd told her.

As Zoey entered the office carrying Rocket in her arms, a nurse in dark blue scrubs rushed to help her.

"Is this Rocket Dawson?" she guessed, signaling another nurse behind the counter to join her.

"Yes."

"My name is Kitty, and this is Leah. While you follow me to the waiting room, she'll take Rocket to the exam room." She nodded to the other nurse, who had already put her hands out to take Rocket, then ushered Zoey to a brown door leading to a narrow room. It had a dark gray bench leaning against the wall and a high chair next to a table.

Kitty asked Zoey some basic questions, like when he'd vomited for the first time and if he could eat or drink. "Do you need some water or tea while you're waiting?" she asked once she had gotten the information she needed.

"No, I'm good. Thank you."

"Okay, please stay here while the vet examines your dog," she told Zoey, taking off and leaving her alone.

As soon as the nurse left, silence reigned and the clock ticking on the wall became deafening. Zoey paced the room, feeling lost. It felt like forever until that door opened again, revealing a familiar man in gray scrubs, carrying a clipboard.

"Hi, Zoey," TJ greeted her. She detected sympathy in his angular eyes.

"How's Rocket, TJ?" Her voice trembled. She didn't want to see her ex-boyfriend, but she couldn't avoid bumping into him here.

"We drew his blood for some tests. The complete blood count and urinalysis look normal, but we're waiting for the results of his biochemistry profile and thyroid hormone testing. Usually, that will take another forty-five minutes." His textured bangs fell across his forehead as he read the information off the clipboard. Zoey remembered brushing her fingers through his thick chestnut hair, now shoulder-length and tied back in a ponytail. "Once we get everything, the vet will talk to you."

"So what's the cause of his vomiting and lost appetite?" asked Zoey.

TJ leaned his back against the table. "I don't want to overstep the vet, especially since the results aren't all back yet. However, since I know the circumstances, I'd guess he's stressed out because he...misses your sister."

A wave of heat welled behind her eyes. Zoey looked away, clenching her jaw, unwilling to cry in front of TJ. "But he'll be okay, though?"

"I think so." TJ pressed the clipboard to his broad chest, sighing. "I'm sorry. I know how important Rocket is to you. But rest assured, I'll keep an eye on him. I promise."

The words broke her defense. Covering her face, Zoey sobbed, her shoulders shaking. "I can't lose him now, TJ."

Pushing away from the table, he exhaled, reached his arm out, and gave her a sideways hug. "Yeah, I know," he whispered.

Zoey sniffed and pulled away, noticing the wetness on TJ's scrubs. "Sorry."

"That's okay. Crying is better than bottling it up." He tapped her shoulder gently, giving her a box of Kleenex.

Zoey took some and dabbed her tears.

"I'm going to leave you now, and the vet will be here once we get the results. But if you need anything, just let me know," TJ said.

"Thanks."

He held her in his gaze for a second before leaving.

Staring at the closed door, Zoey sighed and sat back on the bench. TJ's presence brought comfort and pain—mostly regret—to her heart.

Accompanied by anguish, she had to wait for another forty minutes until a vet came and told her that Rocket's test results had come back normal. The vet had the same assumption as TJ did. She suggested Zoey give him soft food for the time being and said to bring him back if he threw up again within two weeks.

Zoey flinched inwardly when the nurse gave her the bill for today's treatment, and the estimated bill if she were to let Rocket stay in the hospital for twelve hours since he was weak and dehydrated.

"Do I have another option?" she asked Kitty, who also took care of the payment.

"You can try to give him chicken broth and an electrolyte solution for dogs. I'll email you the links. Also, if you want, I can set up for a vet technician to come to your house today to administer an IV. It would be cheaper than an overnight stay here," Kitty said, offering her sympathy. "I'm sorry for your dog, but he'll be better soon."

Zoey bit her lower lip as she listened to the nurse. "I think I'll have the technician come to my house. You already have my address in your file, right?"

Kitty looked at her computer and nodded. "Will you be home at one o'clock?" she asked.

"Yes."

"Great. I'll schedule for someone to come by then."

"Thanks."

The staff here always went the extra mile for their clients, like the nurse who helped Zoey carry the Shiba into her car and made sure she didn't forget the medicines. Zoey understood why her sister hadn't wanted to go to another vet's office.

Zoey was in the living room waiting for a vet technician after feeding Ella. At one o'clock, the doorbell rang. She almost had a heart attack when she saw TJ standing in the front yard.

"The office sent me here," he said sheepishly before Zoey had time to open her mouth.

"Ah, yes, not a problem at all. Please come on in." She held the door open. "Rocket knows you, so that's perfect."

TJ took the IV kits from his backpack in the living room and put them on the coffee table. Rocket recognized him and growled a little, but didn't pull away when TJ inserted a needle into his vein. When he was done wrapping a Velcro catheter guard around Rocket's front leg, the dog licked his hand.

"Do you want some water or a soft drink?" Zoey asked TJ after he washed his hands and was drying them with a paper towel in the kitchen.

"Black coffee would be good. I have a class at two o'clock," he said and then returned to the living room, settling down on the armchair next to Rocket.

Zoey held her breath. Being a vet was TJ's dream, and before breaking up, they'd promised to study together. She'd signed up for CPA preparation courses, and he was planning to get his doctor of veterinary medicine degree. His plan seemed to be going in the right direction, while hers wasn't.

"I only have instant coffee," she said, managing to keep her tone even.

"That's fine. I like any type of coffee," said TJ.

Less than two minutes later, Zoey brought a big blue mug and handed it to him. TJ took it and thanked her. Their fingers brushed as he took the cup from her hand.

Zoey forced a smile and picked Ella up from her little swing before sitting down on the couch. The baby rounded her eyes and stretched her little hand out to TJ. He looked at her, reluctantly moving from his armchair to settle on the sofa next to Zoey. He stayed an arm's length away from her as he took Ella's hand. She shrieked happily.

"She's bigger than the last time I saw her," he said.

"Yes, she gained an ounce this morning," Zoey said, preventing her niece from leaning closer to TJ.

"How are things going? Is everything okay?" he asked, letting Ella hold his finger.

Zoey didn't answer right away. She lowered her head to kiss Ella's, wondering whether she could be honest about how she'd been doing without seeming like a pessimistic Eeyore. But she and TJ had been friends since junior high—he would know if she lied.

"It's tough. I get so overwhelmed when she cries nonstop for no reason," Zoey said, rubbing her temple. She opened up about her problems with Ella, neglecting to mention the frowns she'd received from people who didn't know the real story. After all, the spectators were always the loudest and the fiercest in the arena.

"She also doesn't have a regular sleep schedule yet and wakes up every three or four hours. Her pediatrician says she'll sleep longer hours when she is a bit older. I just hope she can sleep well tonight so I can get some rest."

"I'm sorry it's so hard." TJ kept his gaze trained on her. "Have you considered getting a live-in nanny? At least you'll have someone to help you clean the house and do the grocery shopping. Or help you specifically when Ella wakes up at night."

"That's expensive," Zoey told him. "I'm no longer working, and the money Katya left for the baby is just enough to cover our basic needs and an hourly sitter. I've considered selling more of Katya's stuff, and I don't need the iPhones and Richard's electric guitars. And this house"—Zoey scanned the room, sighing heavily—"has three rooms. I am considering renting one out, but I'm not sure anyone will be interested since there's an infant in the house."

"Can I give you my opinion?" TJ asked.

She nodded.

"If I were you, I wouldn't worry about renting out the room. Focus on your adjustment with Ella. Once you're settled, you can think about it again. But that's up to you, of course."

Although they were nearly the same age, by only a few months difference, Zoey looked at TJ and admired his maturity. Since the day he and Nora had picked her up in Monterey, she'd wondered what would've happened if they were still together now. Would her life be more manageable because she'd have someone to discuss her problems with? Or would he stay away from her and not want to be involved in her household drama?

"Sorry if I offended you." TJ had misunderstood her expression.

"No." Zoey waved her hand in the air. "I think you're right. I shouldn't rush the plan. Thanks."

TJ smiled a little. "Is Lena's replacement helpful? What's her name again? Tangerine? Valencia?"

"Clementine." Zoey smiled and rolled her eyes. "If I had another option, I'd fire her. She's so lazy and forgetful. I miss Lena. I could depend on her."

Maybe Zoey was just imagining the sorrow she saw in TJ's eyes as he leaned forward, clasping his hands together with his elbows on his knees. She lowered her head to blow raspberries on Ella's stomach. The baby let out a high-pitched giggle.

"I like the way she laughs," TJ commented.

"Me too." Zoey smiled and lowered her gaze as their eyes met.

"Well, I've better go now," TJ said, rising to his feet. "Rocket's IV is good until nine o'clock, and I'll be back to replace it. Don't be surprised if he seems lethargic for now. The medicine I injected into his IV will make him sleepy."

"Okay, thanks." Zoey stood up too.

"See you tonight, and thanks for the coffee." TJ grabbed the doorknob, brushing his hair out of his eyes with his other hand, revealing an inch-long stitch mark above his right eyebrow. Zoey knew the story behind that scar by heart.

It had happened in ninth grade when they'd joined the junior counselor's program. During the outdoor activity, she'd tripped near the bamboo grove and TJ had caught her arm in time, but his footing wasn't stable. He'd saved Zoey, but a sharp piece of broken bamboo had caused a laceration above his eyebrow, which had needed two stitches. Zoey never forgot that moment. That was the day she fell in love with him.

"Don't mention it. See you tonight." TJ's words pulled her back. He nodded with his eyes and stepped outside.

Zoey closed the door, holding on to the knob as if searching for any warmth left behind by TJ's fingers.

CHAPTER 4

Sweat broke out on Zoey's forehead as she pushed her shopping cart through the sea of people, as if half of the town had nothing better to do than shop for food on Wednesday morning.

Zoey breathed in. She shifted her eyes from one aisle to another, looking for the baby section. As she reached a section for granola and cold and hot cereal, she saw a cart blocking the cookies with the owner nowhere to be found.

"So inconsiderate," Zoey murmured, feeling fed up, and steered her cart in a different direction.

Most people liked shopping in person because they enjoyed feeling the product they wanted to buy in their hands, but these stores always stressed Zoey out. Too many choices on the shelves, endless versions of a single product. Long checkout lines because only a few counters were open. Inconsiderate people who always let their carts occupy the whole aisle.

Online shopping was the best solution for her. If she had to go in person, she preferred the self-checkout—simple and straightforward. She wanted to do that now but wasn't familiar with this store. Even though she'd moved to this city months ago, she'd never set foot in here before. Lena had done all the work.

Unfortunately, Clementine didn't do the things Lena had, nor had she given Zoey a reminder to order baby formula when she placed a grocery order online last night. This morning, when she went to make milk for Ella, there was only enough to make five ounces. Panic had risen in the pit of her stomach when she found no extra cans in the kitchen cabinet.

Yelling at Clementine was like talking to a wall.

Zoey would be lying if she said she hadn't considered letting Ella drink regular milk. She'd poured some into one of her bottles and pretended to drink from it.

"It's yummy, yummy milk, Ella," she said and licked her lips.

Sucking her pacifier, Ella had looked at her with disinterest in her blue eyes.

So, here she was in a jungle of tall aisles surrounded by other shoppers. Meanwhile, Ella seemed to have inherited her mom's social butterfly personality. She enjoyed being the center of attention and gave passersby a toothless smile as she rocked gently in her cart hammock.

The pharmacy aisle was relatively empty, and Zoey chose to cut down it to the baby section. There she stood, gazing at the shelf of baby formula, when someone called her name.

She turned toward the source. A woman of medium height wearing a green long-sleeve blouse and black pants waved before approaching and stopping in front of her. She smiled, her amber eyes full of warmth.

Zoey didn't recall who she was until the woman said, "I'm Claudia. We met in Green Wood Park last Thursday, remember?"

Zoey now recognized her face, including the small mole below her lips.

"What a surprise to see you here," she said.

"I haven't seen you in the park since we last met. Is everything okay?" asked Claudia.

"Rocket got sick the day after we met, and I haven't been there since then," Zoey explained. "But he's okay now."

"I'm glad. It must be tough to have to take care of him when you have a baby," Claudia said. "Why don't we exchange phone numbers? That way, anytime you need help, you can just call me." She took her phone from her bag and handed it to Zoey.

"It's tough, but I've managed." Zoey typed in her number before returning it to Claudia. "Text me, so I can get yours."

Claudia nodded. A split second later, Zoey's phone buzzed.

"You shop in this store too?" she asked because she remembered Claudia lived in the Kensington apartments on the northern side of the town, about a twenty-minute drive away. There was a similar store in a shopping strip a block away from her place.

"No," said the woman. "I'm here to pick up my neighbor's prescription. She's very sick, and no one in her family lives nearby. I told her to switch her pharmacy to one closer to our apartment, but she kept forgetting and I didn't want to force her. Since I work from home part-time as an online English teacher for international students, I have flexible time and always help my neighbors when they need it."

"Oh, how nice of you," Zoey exclaimed.

"Ah, it's nothing. I have more free time than others." Claudia studied her. "By the way... is that a new hairstyle?" She pointed to Zoey's forehead.

Zoey blinked and felt heat rising in her face as she removed big pink hair rollers from her bangs. No wonder people had been staring at her ever since she pulled into the parking lot.

"Thanks," she mumbled, shoving the rollers into her bag, embarrassed.

"That's okay," Claudia whispered, comforting her. "When my kids were Ella's age, I'd come out of the house with face masks on, hair rollers still in my hair, half my makeup done—you name it." She laughed at the memory, and Zoey laughed with her.

Ella seemed to like her too. When Claudia called her name, she waved her tiny hands at her, smiling and showing her toothless gums. Her drool dribbled down her chin, and Zoey wiped it away with a soft cloth.

"Do you come to this store regularly?" Claudia asked.

"No," said Zoey. "We're here for her baby formula because I miscalculated and thought we still had enough left. I have to buy it now—the online order won't deliver until late in the afternoon."

"I see, but don't be too hard on yourself. That's normal." Zoey saw the sympathy in her eyes before she turned to scan the aisle. "Let me help you. Which one is it that Ella usually drinks? Enfamil? Similac? Gerber? Earth Best? EleCare?"

Zoey pointed to a white can with a baby picture and a blue cloud on it. "That one."

"How many? One or two?"

"One will be enough because I already ordered five cans," said Zoey.

"I don't want to lecture you, but I suggest taking two to give you peace of mind if the shipment is delayed. But it's up to you."

Her advice felt like a fresh breeze in Zoey's tired mind. Since Clementine was unreliable, she didn't have anyone she could share her burdens with, or ask a simple question, like which diapers or pacifiers she should buy for Ella. She could find many of the answers through Google, but preferred to get advice from a real person, since not all of those sites could be trusted.

The support group for young moms Harold had put her in touch with wasn't helpful, rather seemed to just be full of whiners. She'd thought she could find another support group once she had some free time, but it hadn't happened yet. Asking Nora was useless since her best friend had zero baby experience and had been busy helping her parents.

"You're right. I'll take two," Zoey agreed.

Claudia nodded and put two cans in her cart. "Do you need anything else? I can help while I'm here."

"I think I'm good. Thanks," Zoey said.

"Okay, then."

They sauntered toward the cashier, while Claudia stopped to check some items at the gondola or freestanding displays along the way, asking Zoey's opinion about certain items. She didn't mind and realized it was nice to go shopping with a friend.

As they were leaving, Zoey found herself amazed by how imperceptibly the past thirty minutes in the store had gone by, something that never happened when she went shopping alone. It must be because Claudia was such good company. Although she must have experience as a mom, Claudia didn't scrutinize or educate Zoey about caring for infants. Mostly, she talked about her English students.

"See you in the park tomorrow afternoon?" Claudia asked as they were about to part.

"Absolutely. See you tomorrow. We'll be there around four."

"Perfect."

Just as Zoey was about to lower herself into her car seat, someone called her name. She turned to see a man in a white polo shirt and khaki pants waving to her from the curb. He must have just come from the dry cleaner next to the grocery store, as he was holding a bag of freshly laundered shirts.

Her heart danced a little as she recognized Derek Waltz, the handsome stranger who had tamed Ella. It was difficult for Zoey to forget how attractive he'd looked humming and holding her niece in his arms that night. The chemistry between him and the baby was too beautiful to ignore.

Zoey stepped out of her car, leaving the door open as Derek came toward her.

"I didn't know you lived around here," Zoey told him as they stood face-to-face. She took a moment to compose herself, suddenly self-conscious about her house slippers and blue pajama pants. She had panicked about the baby formula and not considered what she was wearing when she rushed to the store.

"I'll be housesitting at my friend's house for the next six months and have been staying there for the past two weeks. It was only then I realized his house isn't far from Katya's house," he replied, peering into the open car door. "How's Ella doing? Did you find out why she was crying so hard?"

Zoey shook her head. "I've been meaning to ask her pediatrician, but since it hasn't happened again, I haven't brought her yet."

"I see. Well, perhaps teething, although I think she's too young for that. Or"—Derek shrugged—"she misses her mom?"

That comment got Zoey's attention. Although Ella was four months old, she might have missed Katya—as Rocket did—considering the deep bond they would have formed during the pregnancy.

"Or she was just cranky for no reason," Derek was quick to add.

"You seem young, but you must've encountered many babies in your life," Zoey teased him.

"I was fifteen when my mom had my triplet brothers. That's where my experience handling babies comes from," Derek said, revealing a dimple Zoey hadn't noticed last time.

"Hey, I'd love to chat more, but I need to feed Ella," she said.

"Sure thing." Derek held the car door for her as she got in. "And don't forget, I'm right nearby, so if you need any help, just give me a howl. Did I already give you my personal number?"

"Yes, I've got it saved in my phone," she lied, although she often forgot to do so.

He smiled. "See you around, Zoey—and Ella." He looked past her in the direction of the baby and then shut her car door.

Derek waited until she put the car in gear and pulled out of the parking lot. In her rearview mirror, Zoey could see him watching as her car rolled slowly toward the street.

CHAPTER 5

Watching Katya from the sidelines, Zoey had understood that having a baby must be tough. But what she'd seen was just the tip of the iceberg. Once she agreed to be Ella's guardian, Zoey had found her life revolved around her. She used to love hanging out at the library, going to the cinema to see a new movie, or eating at her favorite restaurants, but not anymore. She now constantly had to consider Ella when she did or planned things.

Their two-story townhouse was cluttered with baby stuff. Bottles on the kitchen countertop, boxes of diapers in the hallway, a swing, a car seat, a crib, formula—it was never ending.

Zoey was learning new skills too. When Katya was alive, Zoey had never changed Ella's diaper because she couldn't stand the smell. Now, she had become an expert, her nose trained to detect what was in the diaper before even unfastening it.

Nighttime waking and feeding used to be an issue, but now, while half-asleep, Zoey could measure formula and warm it to the perfect temperature or bounce Ella's crib with her big toe.

To maintain her sanity, Zoey initially thought about raising Ella as a challenge she needed to conquer. This faded once everything became repetitive. There was feeding time, nap time, and diaper changes in between, an endless cycle.

Lately, she'd been waking up at dawn, unable to go back to sleep until Ella's morning feeding. Right now she was lying in the dark, staring at the ceiling, remembering her dreams of traveling to lots of countries, learning watercolor painting, running a marathon, starting her career in accounting, and later opening her own CPA firm. Her birthday was approaching, and she thought about the plan she had made with Nora, who would have turned twenty-two that same month. They were going to celebrate her turning twenty-one in a rotating sky lounge at the Strat Hotel in Las Vegas.

"It's expensive, but you only turn twenty-one once," she told Nora, who'd agreed instantly.

But dreams were only dreams. With the baby needing constant care, there was no way she could celebrate in the grand way she'd imagined. Could she achieve her dreams if she gave up her rights as Ella's guardian and let her be adopted by a lovely couple who would spoil her?

Zoey rubbed her face with her hands. She had to keep Ella—she loved her and kept reminding herself that motherhood was a noble thing. But it was also a difficult thing.

Lately, Zoey had been muting her high school and college group chats because she couldn't swallow reading another message saying "I'm engaged," or "I got a job in Google," or "I got a promotion," or even something like "I just broke up with my girlfriend or boyfriend."

None of her classmates understood that a four-month-old baby needed to be fed every three or four hours. They weren't ignorant or mean—they just hadn't had that experience yet.

Although there was a big age difference between them, Claudia Erickson made her life bearable. Zoey felt pure happiness whenever she came home after seeing her. Her new friend didn't judge or ask too many questions. She taught Zoey to appreciate her new life as a sudden mom, celebrating with her when Ella reached milestones like being able to lift her head up when lying on her tummy.

Despite her cheerful manner, Claudia had lived a tough life. Her husband had become abusive once their business failed, and her kids somehow blamed her for everything.

Zoey admired her friend's strong personality and how she had kept herself going. For the past decade, Claudia had worked as an online English teacher for international students, mainly in Asia. Because of the different time zones, she worked primarily in the early morning, while the rest of California was sleeping.

The most significant distraction in Zoey's life, however, was Derek Waltz. The male Mary Poppins mesmerized her with his ability to calm Ella. After their unexpected meeting in front of the grocery store, Zoey wanted to see him again, and her wish came true two days later when her garage door wouldn't open. The springs were broken, and she panicked, not knowing what to do. On a whim, she called and told him about the problem.

Derek came to her house and checked on it. Since it was relatively simple, he offered to fix it, and in less than a half day, the door was working as it should. Derek refused payment, so Zoey bought him dinner at a nearby restaurant. After that, they talked on the phone often, from which she learned he loved traveling and photography.

He had visited her house yesterday to share photos of his recent trip to Montreal and Quebec City and gave her a bag of maple syrup candy from the trip.

Sucking one candy, she listened to Derek's explanation about each photo and admitted that he had a good eye for photography because they had sharp quality and were taken from a unique angle.

She liked photos of the Dufferin Terrace—a long boardwalk with gazebos—wrapped around the most photographed hotel, Fairmont Le Château Frontenac, overlooking the St. Lawrence River. The photos were spectacular, and she imagined herself sitting on one of the gazebos, admiring the scenery.

Pictures of Quartier Petit Champlain and Place Royale offered different sensations in her heart. The cobblestones and old-fashioned facade stores were steeped in history and made her feel as if she had traveled back four hundred years by just looking at them.

She smiled at an adorable video of him and other tourists dancing following the melody of *New York, New York* sang by an old street performer in front of Hotel Manoir Morgan.

As she looked at pictures of him in the Montreal Botanical Garden and Marie-Reine-du-Monde Cathedral, his gentle smile wrapped itself around her heart. It took her some time to recognize the pounding sound coming from her heart.

Zoey might not have had much experience as a mom, but she wasn't ignorant. She saw a flicker in Derek's eyes whenever he gazed at her and knew he was interested. And she was interested in him. She didn't remember when she began feeling that way. Perhaps it had started when he comforted Ella on that stressful night.

He made her laugh and forget about the problems in her life. He was considerate and understood how hard it was to take the baby to a store or restaurant. Whenever he knew Zoey hadn't cooked, he would buy her food from restaurants and drop it off at her place. A few times, he bought more and ate with her. It gave Zoey a real break from frozen meals and a chance to have a pleasant conversation during dinner.

Claudia and Derek were godsends.

The wound in her heart from losing her sister was still raw after being thrown into sudden motherhood and, later, forced to give up her job. She'd felt miserable and doubted whether she'd have a love life again, but everything changed. Her doubt faded, and she finally felt her life become meaningful and cheerful again.

CHAPTER 6

Clementine was troublesome and cunning. She came to work whenever she wanted because she knew that without her help, Zoey's life would be miserable.

It was true, Zoey needed her. It had been weeks, and she'd had to control her emotions, not saying a word whenever Clementine called in sick. Zoey thought she was simply lazy. Five days earlier, she'd finally lost her patience and told Clementine to stop coming, but it backfired.

The house was now chaotic and smelled bad. The trash can was overflowing. There were dirty bottles in the sink because the dishwasher was broken, and Zoey didn't have time to contact a handyman to help her fix it. Empty boxes of frozen food and canned food were lying everywhere.

When Zoey needed to change her clothes, she took fresh ones directly from the dryer because she didn't have time to hang them in her closet. The dark circles under her eyes from lack of sleep were noticeable. Rocket's walks grew shorter, but at least he didn't lack for food or water, thanks to the automatic food and water dispensers that had certainly been worth the money.

Zoey should've searched for her replacement before firing Clementine, but the milk was already spilled now. Furthermore, as an introverted person, she didn't have many friends to ask for help. Derek was on a business trip to San Francisco for a week. Claudia was in town, but she was attending an ESL teacher conference. Nora couldn't come since she worked full-time. However, Nora's mom had called and told Zoey that her friend's daughter—a seventeen-year-old girl with first aid and CPR certifications—was interested in babysitting twice a week for two hours. Zoey accepted immediately and found bliss in those two-hour windows.

One morning, Harold called to check on her. "You sound so tired. What happened?" he asked.

Her nose burned as she felt heat pooling behind her eyes. She stammered as she explained her situation to the attorney.

"Didn't I tell you to call me whenever you need help?" replied Harold. "Don't worry. I'll tell my executive assistant to find you another permanent nanny quickly. In the meantime, we can contact childcare agencies that can provide a same-day temporary one. It'll be costly, but it should be fine for a short time."

"I can't pay too much," reminded Zoey.

"Yes, I understand. I'll make sure the price will be in your budget," he replied, calming her.

"By the way, thanks for letting Derek help me, Harold. He's been so useful," said Zoey.

"Uh...I'm not sure I follow you, dear." He sounded confused.

"Derek Waltz. Isn't he working for you?" Zoey breathed.

"Derek...yes, he used to work for me, but not anymore. Why do you ask?"

"Oh, he came over to give me his condolences," Zoey said quickly. Had Derek lied to her? If so, why?

"I see. Yes, he knew Katya, but he is no longer working with me," Harold confirmed. "Anyway, is there anything else I can help you with? If not, I should hang up now because I have a client in five minutes."

"Okay, thanks for checking on me, Harold."

"Take care, Zoey."

She frowned as she put the phone down, but her thought was interrupted by the doorbell. When she peered through the peephole, she saw Claudia standing on the patio holding two reusable shopping bags.

"Hey there." Claudia smiled as Zoey opened the door. "Your Amazon Fresh has also arrived." She pointed to the brown bags on the patio, but her smile fell when she saw her friend's face. "Is everything okay?" she asked hesitantly. "Maybe I'll come back later."

"No." Zoey shook her head. "Just come in, but ignore the mess."

Claudia's eyes grew round as she stepped inside, but she composed herself quickly. "Let me put these in your kitchen." She held up the bags she was carrying. "And bring your grocery bags in."

Shame washed over Zoey as Claudia pushed aside an empty can of baby formula and an open box of chicken pot pie to make room on the countertop. Then she walked past her to bring the Amazon Fresh bags to the kitchen.

Claudia turned to her. "Why don't you sit and rest on the couch? And I'll make you some tea with honey if you tell me where you keep them."

"The second cabinet from the right, and the teapot is on the stove." Zoey's voice trembled as she brought a shaky hand to her forehead. She was tired, body and soul, and let Claudia lead her to the sofa. Ella might have sensed something was happening because she woke up and became fussy.

"Oh no, I woke you up." Zoey picked Ella up from the swing. "Shhh…Shhh…Don't cry, baby. Why are you crying? Did an itsy-bitsy ant bite you? But you're bigger than the ant."

Ella's crying stopped as Zoey bounced her gently. She pressed her little forehead to Zoey's chest and clenched her shirt, making a soft bubbly noise.

A few minutes later, Claudia brought back a cup of tea and put it on the coffee table in front of Zoey. "Why don't you drink it while it's still warm and let me hold Ella?"

"Thanks." She handed the baby over. A thin smile broke on her lips when her niece burst into peals of laughter as Claudia bounced her on her lap.

"Would you care to tell me what happened?" Claudia asked.

Zoey looked down at the cup in her hands. For a while, the only sounds in the room were her voice and Ella's coos.

"I'm sorry for what you've been through," her friend said once she was finished. "As you know, I work part-time. My students live on a different continent, mostly in Asia, and with the time difference, I usually start teaching at nine in the evening and go until five in the morning. Most of the time, I only have two or three classes, with a recess in between. Usually, after teaching, I don't sleep until seven in the morning and wake up at three in the afternoon. My work days are mostly Fridays, weekends, and Mondays. If you don't mind, I can help you until you find a permanent nanny."

"I can't pay you much, Claudia. Besides, will you be okay staying here? What about your apartment?"

"I live with my best friend. Her daughter is visiting from Korea in two days and will stay a while because she has to attend some college open houses here. If you let me help you, it'd be perfect timing. My friend and her daughter would have more freedom in the apartment without me around," Claudia explained, laying

Ella on the couch. "Don't worry about paying me. I'd be grateful if you could buy my food and let me use the internet connection for teaching. Try me for two nights, and if you don't feel comfortable, just let me know."

Zoey's stomach clenched. She wanted to say yes, but she was afraid that if something didn't go well, it would affect their friendship and she liked talking to her.

Claudia caught her hesitation. "Listen to me. Ella needs you. If you don't take care of yourself, who will?"

"I know." Zoey exhaled. "Okay, let's try it for two days."

"Sounds good."

Zoey forced a thin smile and was distracted by a movement on her right side. Ella had rolled onto her tummy and pushed herself up on her elbows. Her blue eyes looked straight into Zoey's.

Zoey couldn't believe it. "Claudia, look," she whispered, pointing with her eyes.

"Oh my." The older woman put a hand over her mouth. "How old is she now?"

"She is..." Zoey thought for a moment. "Wow, she's already five months. I totally forgot." She rubbed Ella's soft hair lovingly.

The baby giggled and rolled over to lie on her back again.

"Hey, why don't we celebrate this milestone?" Claudia clasped her hands together. "I happened to buy a half-dozen strawberry croissants from a Japanese bakery on my way over here, as well as a fresh rotisserie chicken, Hawaiian rolls, and asparagus soup. Do you think that's enough for us? If not, I don't mind buying more from a restaurant nearby."

"I think that's plenty." Zoey looked at her beaming face. "Thanks."

"Anytime. Now, you sit here and relax while I make us some plates." Claudia rose to her feet.

"The plates and forks are in the first and second drawers." Zoey was touched by her enthusiasm. If she hadn't met Claudia, who would she have shared her excitement with?

CHAPTER 7

Claudia had been helping Zoey for three days. In that short time, her presence had brought positive change, giving Zoey time to do some errands and clean.

The house was less messy and smelled deliciously of food Claudia cooked using whatever ingredients she found in the fridge. She didn't listen when Zoey forbade her to cook because she wasn't paying her to. Rather than arguing, Zoey let her friend do it and bought more ingredients whenever she went to the grocery store.

There was always a simple breakfast ready on the kitchen counter when she woke up: toast or fluffy pancakes, boiled or scrambled eggs, and orange juice. Zoey had almost forgotten how delicious homemade food was, especially after eating cold cereal and milk every morning. Rocket liked Claudia—she cooked for him too—and began to shadow her like he had done with Katya.

"Have you eaten a taco pie yet?" Claudia called from the kitchen as she unpacked several grocery bags.

"No, I haven't. Why do you ask?" Zoey came over, tying the end of her braid with an elastic.

"Because we've got a pound of ground beef, green onions, and green pepper in Santa's bags," she answered. Since Zoey had told her friend that she didn't know who was sending her groceries every week, Claudia had taken to calling the benefactor "Santa."

Zoey chuckled. "Okay, taco pie sounds good for dinner."

"And lunch," Claudia added, looking at Zoey's light gray dress. "Ready to go to the cemetery?"

"Yes." Last night Zoey had asked Claudia if she could babysit Ella longer than usual, since she wanted to visit Katya. Luckily, Claudia didn't teach on Thursdays, so she was happy to help.

"Don't forget to buy sunflowers for her."

"Yes, I'll stop at the florist on the way there." Zoey raised an eyebrow. "How did you know her favorite flowers?"

Claudia pointed to a picture of Katya standing beside some giant sunflowers in a botanical garden. There was a caption underneath it that read, "My favorite flowers."

Zoey chuckled. "Yeah, she was crazy about them."

"I'll take Ella and Rocket to Green Wood Park," Claudia said. "Don't be alarmed if you come home and don't see us."

"Thanks. See you later."

On the way to the front door, Zoey quickly kissed Ella and tapped Rocket's fluffy head. The Shiba followed her briefly, then stood near the door, watching her close it.

It took Zoey thirty-seven minutes to drive from her townhouse to the memorial garden where Katya's and Richard's ashes had been interred. She parked and walked through the entrance, rows of columbaria in mahogany-colored granite coming into sight after about five minutes. As she'd expected, the garden was quiet, as most visitors came on weekends.

When she reached the columbarium's last row, her phone pinged in her bag, loud in the quiet surroundings. She picked it up and saw Nora's name on the display.

"Hey, girl," she answered, still walking.

"Are you at Katya's columbarium?" Nora asked.

"Mhm. Thanks for visiting her yesterday."

"Don't mention it. She's my *eonni* too. I miss talking with her."

Nora was an only child and had loved hanging out with Katya. Frequently, she called her *eonni*—older sister in Korean. Zoey didn't mind sharing her sister with her best friend but was jealous of their closeness, especially when they watched and talked about Korean dramas, something that she didn't enjoy. She felt left out whenever they watched films at a CGV cinema in Buena Park that mostly played Korean movies.

"Yeah, me too." Zoey pushed her hand into her pocket, gazing beyond the array of granite for a moment. "Hey, I'm close. I have to hang up now. Talk to you later."

There were two flower arrangements in front of Katya's and Richard's niches. Zoey put the sunflowers between them before sitting down on the cement bench facing the monument. Her reflection was clear on the reddish-brown shiny surface of it.

She breathed out and looked at the blue sky, wondering what her sister was doing on the other side. Could she see everything that happened in her sister's life from above?

If that were so, what would she feel to see her spic-and-span house cluttered?

What was her opinion about her sister's chaotic life only becoming stable after meeting Claudia, who now helped care for Ella and Rocket?

Would she feel joyful knowing that Derek, who had always helped her sister, now showed interest in her regardless of her situation?

Or would she feel upset if she knew that TJ had a new girl-friend, considering Katya used to value him highly among Zoey's male friends?

How Zoey wished Katya could answer those questions and show her a way to find their mom because she was no longer holding a grudge toward her and aching to know where she had been and why she'd left them.

Her reverie was interrupted by her phone ringing, showing Harold's office number. He must've found a permanent nanny. Although Zoey would have preferred to keep Claudia, her job was teaching, not looking after an infant.

"Good morning, Harold."

"Morning, Zoey." His voice was energetic. "Where are you now?"

"I'm at my sister's columbarium. Why?"

"Could you come down to the police station in Santa Ana? They've found the hit-and-run driver."

Zoey felt her knees wobble. Good thing she was sitting down. Finally, after eighty-one days, they had caught the person who killed her sister.

"Did he or she confess?" asked Zoey.

"Well…" There was a pause on the other end. "That person wants to talk to you."

"W-what for? D-did that person know me?" she stammered.

"Why don't you come, Zoey? Once you're there, ask for Joe Rodriguez, the detective who's handling Katya's case."

"Okay. Santa Ana precinct, right? See you there." She hung up, tightening her fingers around the phone. Anger, sadness, and relief mixed in her chest. Although she was glad they'd found who did it, nothing could bring back her sister.

Zoey's eyes were blurry as she looked back at Katya's vault. "Kat, did you hear that? Harold said the police found the person who killed you, but they want to talk to me. I'm so nervous. It's worse than having a job interview. Please watch over me." She clasped her hands together.

The police station was an hour's drive away. Walking up the stairs to the entrance, Zoey gripped the strap of her cross-body bag, comforting herself. She stuttered as she spoke to the front desk officer in the lobby. Her heart pounded hard, and her chest hurt as she was ushered to a large room containing a long table with eight chairs around it.

"Don't worry. You're safe here," the officer comforted her. "Your lawyer is here too, but he's talking to the head detective now. Do you want any water or soda?"

"W-water will be fine."

The officer nodded and left. She quickly returned with a cold bottle and gave it to Zoey before leaving her alone.

Less than five minutes later, the door opened again. Harold and a tall, sturdy officer with tan skin entered the room. Two more men stepped in behind them. A croak escaped Zoey's lips when she saw TJ standing beside Harold and the two policemen. His long brown hair was messy, and not a muscle moved on his face when he saw her.

"TJ? Is that you? W-why are yo...?" Her voice trailed off. She put a hand over her mouth and shook her head hard. Suddenly, something snapped inside her as the pieces fell into place. She remembered the deadly F-150 driver had long hair like TJ's hair.

Reaching her arms out, Zoey jumped at him, but a pair of hands wrapped around her waist from behind, stopping her from clawing at his face. "Why? Why did you do it? My sister liked you, TJ. She even blamed me for breaking up with you. Why did you kill her? Why?"

"Zoey, calm down." It was Harold who was holding her.

She forced herself to turn her head, gawking at him. She tasted bitterness coming up from her throat. "He killed my sister, Harold. My *only* sister. Because of him, we're orphans, me and Ella. How dare you stop m—"

"He *isn't* the driver!" Harold raised his voice.

Zoey stopped thrashing, and her jaw dropped. "What did you say?"

"He isn't the driver," Harold repeated slowly. "Now, please calm down, will you?"

Zoey nodded, staggering as Harold released her from his grip. She stared at TJ, who looked everywhere but at her. His jaw was set, his eyes cold and hard.

"Sit." Harold put his hand on her shoulder.

She slammed down into her seat as TJ took an empty chair two seats away from her. Before anyone had time to explain what was going on, the door opened again. The officer who had given her a drink entered again with a man in a suit, his hands cuffed behind his back.

Zoey blinked. Her heart seemed to freeze midbeat as her eyes grew wider.

The man in the suit was Derek Waltz.

CHAPTER 8

Hugging her big Pikachu plushy, Zoey sat in the dark in her walk-in closet, the door locked from the inside. As a person responsible for raising a baby, she knew her act was childish, but she wanted to be alone for once. Her mind was spinning thinking about what had happened at the police station three hours earlier.

Derek Waltz, the man who had captured her heart with his gentleness toward Ella, had been driving the stolen F-150 that killed her sister. From his confession, she knew he'd held a deep grudge against Katya because she was the person who'd caused Harold to fire him.

Derek had a gambling addiction and constantly needed money. He'd kept borrowing from his family and friends, and eventually, from a loan shark, paying high interest.

When he worked for the law firm, he'd learned that Harold was an eccentric who didn't like electronic payments. All office expenses were paid using checks, cash, or debit cards, including his employees' salaries. Most of his clients paid for his services by check too.

Harold was brilliant and well-liked. He wasn't greedy and felt satisfied if he could help his clients. That was why he kept his office small, with only four employees, including himself.

Derek had known where his boss kept his business checks. He'd also seduced the receptionist, who doubled as a billing clerk. No one noticed the first time he took some money, or the second time, or the third time. Derek became bolder and began to forge checks.

One day, Katya had stopped by Harold's office for an impromptu meeting. Harold had an appointment with a client outside the office, so Derek had snuck into his room and Katya had found him there. As Harold's paralegal, being in his office wasn't unusual for Derek. However, suspicion flashed in Katya's eyes when she picked up a blank check bearing Harold's stamped signature— from a stamp the paralegal had just accidentally dropped. Two weeks later, Harold fired him.

Derek had been unable to pay off his loan or the interest. The loan shark rewarded him by badly beating him, making sure to leave no bruises on his face, legs, or arms.

Anger consumed him. Somehow, he'd heard about Katya's plan to go to Mammoth Lakes and thought he would pay her back for her nosiness. Wearing a wig as camouflage, Derek stole the F-150 and followed Katya's car. On a deserted stretch of the SR-14, he waited for her to come out of a rest stop and slammed into her Lexus. He'd just wanted to scare her, but things turned ugly. After hitting her car three times, Katya lost control and the car spun one-hundred-eighty degrees, hitting the road divider and spinning again before rolling over. It happened in the blink of an eye.

Derek left his truck to check on them. Richard was already dead, his head covered in blood. Derek thought Katya had been killed too, but when he looked at the backseat, he saw her lying there in an awkward position, dying. Through the broken window, he heard her sing a song for Ella who was whimpering and saw how she'd used her body to protect the baby, and that action touched his heart. Regret washed over him. Using his burner phone, he placed an anonymous nine-one-one call, then ran away.

Later, he tried to pay for his sin by visiting Katya's house and helping with Ella. He wasn't interested in Zoey but wanted her to trust him and made the mistake of giving her his business card from when he'd worked for Harold. He didn't know that Zoey had told Harold about him, and his former boss later traced him—with assistance from TJ, who had worked hard to find the deadly F-150 driver.

Zoey felt nauseous. How could she have fallen in love with Derek just because he looked attractive when holding Ella and had tamed her with his song? With the song he only knew about because he'd heard it from her dying sister? She felt ashamed for having fantasized about raising the baby with him.

A knock on the door jolted her out of her thoughts.

"Go away! Leave me alone!" Zoey yelled in frustration.

"Zoey, it's me. Please come out, dear." It was Claudia. "Hiding won't solve anything."

Her gentle voice broke the barrier that had kept Zoey's tears in. She buried her face in the Pikachu to muffle her cries.

"If you won't, I'll stay here with you," she said again. As if reading Zoey's mind, she continued, "Don't worry—Ella is sleeping now."

Sniffing, Zoey heard a soft grunt and pictured Claudia lowering herself onto the carpet outside the closet. Her friend had difficulty sitting on the ground because of her knee. Zoey didn't have the heart to let her stay there for long, and drying her tears with her sleeve, unlocked and opened the door.

"Don't sit there. It's bad for you." She reached down to take her friend's arm to pull her up.

Claudia studied Zoey's face as they sat down on the edge of the bed. "I'm sorry about what happened to you. Derek seemed like a good man," she said softly.

"I must be cursed, Claudia." Zoey choked on her own words and was quick to brush away her tears. "I keep losing people I love. My dad passed away when I turned seven. Two weeks later, my mom left us. Then Grannie Evie died. I broke up with TJ for a man who didn't care about me. Then I lost Katya and Richard. Now, when I thought I had finally found someone to share my life with, it was just another illusion. He killed Kat." She dropped her shoulders. Her tears fell, leaving dark stains on her pants as she lowered her head.

"Hush, don't say that," Claudia chided gently, wrapping her arm around Zoey's shoulder. "No one is cursed. You're blessed."

Zoey shook her head. "If I were blessed, my dad wouldn't have taken drugs, and my mom wouldn't have left Katya and me when we needed her most. She must've hated me because she hasn't tried to find us. She didn't even show up for Katya's funeral. I'm destined to be alone."

"Ah, my dear. Your mom loves you. You know that." Claudia hugged Zoey tightly. Her voice croaked. "Perhaps she's afraid of seeing you. She may think you're still mad at her for leaving you like that. Don't you think so?"

Zoey didn't want to consider that. Her breath came out shaky as she eased away from Claudia and stood up. "It's been a long day. I have a headache, and I'm tired. It's better if I rest now so I can wake up early to feed Ella."

"Just sleep in, Zoey. It's okay—I'll take care of her and Rocket." Claudia stood next to her.

A sad smile broke on Zoey's face as she gave her friend a quick hug. "Thanks for helping me. I don't know what would happen if you weren't here."

"Sleep tight, dear." Claudia's eyes were glassy as she squeezed Zoey's shoulder and walked toward the door. She gazed at her before turning off the light and left.

Zoey was emotionally drained. Her mind was tired too. She dreamed disconnected snippets—scenes from her childhood house, dancing with Katya in the rain, and TJ stealing a kiss in a movie theater near campus.

The flowery visions turned dark as she found herself in a funeral home where three coffins stood: her dad, Katya, and Richard. She saw a little version of herself crying on the curb, then Katya's bleeding face.

Zoey felt a warm hand brush her forehead and heard a voice call her name. In a sleepy fog, she opened her heavy eyes to see a blonde woman bending over her, smiling. "Mom?" she whispered, but the fatigue pulled her back into slumber.

CHAPTER 9

The house was quiet as Zoey went down to the kitchen. The humming of the dishwasher and the crashing and tumbling sound from the fridge embraced her. No sign of Rocket or Claudia. They must be at the park again because Rocket's leash was missing from the hook beside her car key on the kitchen wall.

Zoey ate the breakfast Claudia had prepared and took some painkillers for her headache. She was about to head up to take a shower when her phone rang.

"Hi, Harold." She put the speaker to her ear as she climbed the stairs.

"Hi, Zoey. How are you?" His voice was deep and warm.

"Exhausted."

"Yes, I would be too," he said apologetically. "I have something to tell you. Would you mind meeting me at my office now?"

"Um." Zoey held the railing. "Okay. In an hour would be fine?"

"Perfect."

She quickly rinsed off and got dressed. Claudia hadn't returned home by the time she was leaving and didn't pick up the phone when Zoey called her. The woman was friendly and must be talking to people she'd met in the park. Zoey left a message to tell her where she would be.

When she got to Harold's office, it was quiet as usual. The receptionist ushered her in once she arrived.

"Please sit down," the attorney said once they were face-to-face.

"Thanks." She took a seat. "Could you tell me why you wanted me to come?"

Harold nodded. Folding his hands on the table, he began. "You might not know it, but I've known your family for over two decades. I helped your Grandma Evie write her will, giving you and your sister the house. I also helped Katya in every way I could. I was there when you both were born. I was also there when the police found your dad's body at the dump and—"

He stopped all of a sudden, studying Zoey.

"And?"

"That means I also knew your mom."

"Okay, that makes sense." Zoey gave a light shrug. Talking about her mom brought back the unusual dream she'd had last night. It had been so vivid, as if her mom was in the room with her.

"She contacted me because she wants to meet you."

Zoey's mouth fell open. "What?"

Harold repeated the sentence.

"Wait…" Zoey leaned forward. "Do you know where she's been?"

The attorney nodded. "I know where she lives."

She blinked. "What? Why haven't you told me?"

"In my defense, I wanted to, but Katya forbade me."

"W-wait a minute. Katya knew about her too?"

"Yes. Why don't you sit back, dear?" Harold suggested. Once Zoey settled in her seat, he continued. "From what your sister told me, your mom showed up a few times, but Katya kept refusing her, until her wedding day."

"Why didn't she tell me?"

"She might have had concerns about it."

Zoey bit her trembling lip, remembering something. "M-maybe that's what s-she wanted to tell me before her trip."

Harold tilted his head. "Maybe," he said slowly. The look in his gray eyes was kind. "I'm so sorry. But now that you know your mom wants to meet you, are you willing to see her?"

Zoey's jaw tightened as she nodded. "Where and when?"

"She's already in the other room. Come on. Follow me." He stood up.

Zoey felt fuzzy but didn't say a word. She rose from her seat and followed Harold. They walked down a narrow corridor with big windows overlooking greenery on the left and rows of bookshelves on the right wall. When they came to the second door, Harold stopped and knocked.

"Come on in," a woman answered from inside.

Zoey's heart pounded against her ribcage as Harold turned the doorknob, but then he stopped, turning his head to her.

"Your mom is inside," he said. "I know you might think you're entitled to scream at her after she abandoned you for years, but remember, this is a lawyer's office, not some TV studio. Please behave like a grown-up and let her tell you her story. Can you do that?"

A few years back, she wouldn't have listened to him, but she had changed, even compared to who she'd been a couple months ago. Having Ella had made her into a more mature woman.

Zoey nodded, curling her fingers. "Okay."

Harold held the door, and she entered a meeting room with a long table and comfy chairs. There was a big flat screen TV on the far wall, but Zoey gaze was drawn to the blonde, short-haired woman in a green long-sleeve blouse and black pants. She stood near the window with her back facing them.

"She's here, Abby," Harold called to her.

Abby? Was that my mom's name?

The woman turned around. Her face tensed and the gaze in her blue eyes was furtive as she moved slowly closer to her. "Hello, Zizi."

Zoey froze.

Zizi.

The nickname emerged sluggishly from the deepest part of her memory. Her mom used to call her that a long, long time ago.

Zoey squinted at her mother, who was now standing in front of her. The blonde hair and blue eyes were just as she remembered, but there was something odd about this woman. The way she stood, moved, and even her dress seemed familiar. Then Zoey noticed the tiny black mole on the corner of her lower lip, and it hit her like a punch to the gut. In her mind, she changed the woman's hair to brown and her eyes from blue to amber.

"C-Claudia?"

Claudia, or Abby, as Harold had called her, stood tall and nodded.

"W-why?" Zoey asked, her voice barely above a whisper. She staggered to her feet, swaying a little.

"Sit down, dear. Let your mom explain everything," Harold said from behind her. She'd almost forgotten he was there. "You too, Abby. Please take a seat."

Mom and daughter took seats opposite each other. The tips of Zoey's fingers were cold as she wrung them together for comfort.

"Now, I'll leave you both alone, but I'll be on the other side of the room, watching through that double-pane window." Harold pointed at the rectangular glass at the far end of the room.

Zoey nodded, but her eyes were on Claudia.

"Thanks, Harold," Claudia said.

Once Harold closed the door, the silence in the room grew. Zoey had told people that she didn't care about her mom anymore, but she'd secretly yearned to meet her again and had rehearsed questions she wanted to ask if she ever had a chance to. Her mom was before her now, but Zoey's mind and tongue were numb.

All of a sudden, Zoey pushed her chair back. "Ella? Rocket?" Her eyes scanned the room before they shifted to the woman in front of her. "Where are they?" she demanded.

"I dropped them off at Laurel's office before I drove here," said Claudia, her voice calm.

"Laurel?" Zoey knitted her eyebrows in, sitting back. "As in Laurel Wang Jensen, TJ's mom?"

Claudia nodded. "She doesn't mind watching them while I'm here."

"I didn't know you guys were friends," Zoey muttered.

"We met a few months ago, and yes, she's my good friend now." Zoey looked down, gazing at her hands.

"You can ask me anything, Zizi. I'm ready," Claudia reminded her.

Zoey lifted up her head, looking straight at her blue eyes. "Your last name is Erickson. Is that your new husband's name?"

"No, I haven't remarried. That's just a random name I picked."

Zoey nodded. She breathed in, trying to calm the thunder in her chest. "W-why did you leave me that day?"

Claudia's face was pale, and her eyes grew shiny as she opened her mouth. "You might not remember because you were so young, but I was weak and very self-conscious about my image," she began. "When our business failed, we had to sell our house in Beverly Hills and move to this suburb. Nothing wrong with it, but I felt people were mocking me wherever I went. Your dad and

I fought a lot. We blamed each other, and he turned to drugs. I should've stopped him, but I didn't. I used it too because I wanted to run away from my life.

"Your sister was fourteen when she found me high in the garage. She was upset and confronted me, but I ignored her. Until..." Claudia stopped. Her jaw clasped as she looked beyond the closed door and walls. "The police came to the house and told me your dad had died from an overdose. They found his body in the dump behind the grocery store where he worked. At that moment, I knew I had to seek help. I signed up for rehab, but I had to stay in a closed facility. I should have told you and Katya the truth, but I was a coward. I preferred to have you hate me for abandoning you over being known as an addict.

"My mom—Grandma Evie—knew and agreed to take care of you on my behalf as I sought treatment. She promised not to say anything about my condition. I missed you and your sister badly, but it took me years to return to normal life." Claudia swallowed, rubbing the bridge of her nose. "My mentor in rehab signed me up to volunteer with a women's group at a local church. TJ's mom is the head of it. The day you graduated from college, she saw me watching you from a distance. I—"

"Y-you were there?" Zoey interrupted.

Abby, or Claudia, as she'd known her, took a phone from her bag and scrolled until she found what she wanted. "Here." She pushed it over to Zoey. "The picture isn't very sharp since I took it from a distance."

Zoey scanned the image and saw herself smiling widely with TJ's arm around her shoulders, Nora and Jared on her left side, and two other classmates on the right. Without saying anything, she pushed the phone back to Claudia, who wrapped her fingers around it and continued her story.

"I attempted to talk to Katya, but she kept refusing me until I explained it to her, as I'm doing with you right now. I asked if she could prepare you before I showed up, but she was worried about how you'd react, since you usually clammed up whenever she mentioned me. She meant to tell you before the trip, but it didn't happen."

"But why didn't you show up to Katya's funeral?" Zoey barked, her grief apparent in her voice.

"I was there, but you didn't know it," Claudia said, rather loudly. She let out a sigh and shifted in her seat. "I was the woman who stood beside you when her casket went into the cremation chamber. I hugged you, and you cried on my shoulder." Her voice became gentler.

Recalling the moment, Zoey felt her breath become ragged. "That person...was you?" she whispered.

"Yes."

Zoey pursed her lips and looked up to the ceiling, blinking furiously.

Claudia exhaled again, rubbing her fingers together anxiously.

"So, are you also the one behind the Santa bags?" Zoey asked after a long pause.

"I wish, Zizi, but I live on a tight budget."

"But you didn't seem surprised by them. Is that because you know who the sender is?"

"Yes, that's TJ."

Zoey's lips parted. "You know him?"

Claudia nodded. "His mom invited the women's group to have lunch at her house. TJ happened to be there. Since Laurel knew about my relationship with you, she introduced us. I asked him questions about you, and he mentioned the bags in passing.

"TJ helped me get close to you, aware of the pain you were in because of me. Showing up at your front door as your mom wouldn't have been a good idea. Being your friend seemed much better. TJ suggested I bump into you at one of the parks near your house. The problem was that we didn't know which one you'd go to. I checked all three of them almost daily until you finally arrived at Green Wood. I was sorry to hear what Clementine did to you, but I was happy for the opportunity when you started looking for a new nanny."

She looked Zoey in the eyes. "Zizi, I've hurt you badly. I'm sorry. How I wish I hadn't been too much of a coward to tell you the truth. I can't change the past, but I can change the future if you let me. If you don't want me as your mom, that's okay too, but let me be your friend," Claudia said.

Zoey pinched her thigh a few times to keep from crying. Obviously, the universe liked joking around because deep in her heart, she'd wished Claudia was more than her friend. Now, she was overwhelmed by the facts thrown before her.

"Zoey," Claudia said after a while. "Will you forgive me?" Her voice thickened.

The grief on her face tugged at Zoey's heartstrings.

"If I hadn't forgiven you, I wouldn't have bothered listening to your explanation," she said, her eyes becoming cloudy.

CHAPTER 10

The meeting at the attorney's office had ended well, but Zoey's interactions with Claudia became awkward at home. Her heart fluttered with happiness, but she was cautious at the same time. It was hard to break the invisible wall she'd built around her heart over the years.

The word *Mom* never came out of her mouth, but Claudia didn't seem to care what Zoey called her. She was still cheerful, always sitting at the table, holding Ella while she waited for Zoey to eat her meal.

Zoey felt reluctant about seeing TJ, even though everything in her life had fallen into the right place because of him. The problem was she didn't know how to thank him because she felt ashamed of having broken up with him without saying anything. She knew the reason, but she couldn't articulate it.

One late afternoon, she waited for him in the parking lot of the pet hospital, holding an iced coffee. Her heart thundered in her ears as the back door opened. Wearing a striped shirt, TJ slung his backpack on his left shoulder, his right hand fiddling with the car key as he sauntered to his car. He didn't see her as he unlocked it and threw his bag in.

"TJ," Zoey called. Her voice must have been too soft, as TJ opened the driver's side door without looking up. "TJ!" she yelled again.

He stiffened and turned in her direction. A little smile broke on his lips. "Hey, Zoey. What a surprise."

He stood there, raising an eyebrow as she walked closer.

"You cut your hair." She pointed.

"Yeah, long hair made me itchy."

Zoey chuckled and thrust the coffee at him. "Here."

"What is it?" He glanced at it without taking it.

"Medium iced café latte, no sugar," she answered, waving the cup. "Don't worry—I didn't put anything bad in it."

TJ took it, but his eyes were on Zoey, who buried her hands in the pockets of her pants. "What's it for?"

"My simple thank for your help," Zoey swallowed, biting her lip. The words she'd practiced earlier were gone with the wind. Clearing her throat, she continued. "Harold told me about how you tried to find the culprit through social media. Without your help, we never would have found him." She felt a soft tug in her heart whenever she thought of Derek. She let out a breath. "Also, for the Amazon Fresh. You shouldn't have done it, you know."

TJ gave a casual shrug, but blushed briefly and clicked his tongue. "Abby told you."

"Claudia. I've known her as Claudia," she corrected him.

"Fair enough." He nodded and took a gulp of the latte, which must have been lukewarm by now.

"The food has helped me a lot, but I hope you stop sending it. I'll be sad if someone misunderstands your intentions."

TJ tilted his head. "Who would do that?"

"Should I say it out loud?"

"Maybe." He shrugged. "Because I don't think I follow you." Holding the cup, he crossed his arms over his chest.

Zoey exhaled and almost rolled her eyes. "Your girlfriend. I don't want your girlfriend to be upset with me."

"Hmm, let me think," he said. "The last time I checked, my girlfriend broke up with me for someone else without telling me why."

"Not funny." Zoey frowned. "I saw you come out from the new dine-in cinema with your arm around her. She's pretty and you guys look good together."

"Ah, that one." TJ gave an exaggerated nod. "That's why I don't like going out with my cousin whenever she visits us."

Zoey felt her jaw drop. "She's your cousin? I thought I'd met all your cousins."

"You haven't met Rose yet because she lives in New Zealand. When she visited last time, we had already broken up." He put the latte on the roof of his car and took two steps closer to her, his expression solemn. "I don't have a girlfriend, and I hope you understand my feelings for you by now. They haven't changed, and they won't until I decide to change them, which is not likely. You hurt me when you broke up with me because you didn't give me any reason. That bothered me. It took me weeks to understand why you did that, but later, I understood that I'd indirectly taken part in your decision. Given your circumstances, I should have known what you expected from a boyfriend. You'd rather move on than hang out with a man who just wants to enjoy life and never thinks seriously about his future. I'm sorry. I—" TJ looked down to the ground before lifting his eyes. "I must have hurt your feelings when I said you'd rather spend your time working than with me. I'm so insensitive. I'm so dense. I'm sorry, Z."

"That's okay, TJ." Zoey gave him a little smile. "I was too uptight back then. Perhaps my fear of becoming a burden on Katya affected my decision, too. For a decade, she kept me under her wing, and I didn't like that. I wanted to release her from being my mom. That's why I tried so hard to establish my career and began to save money for my future."

For a few moments, they stood facing each other in silence. The confession seemed to have awoken a fragile, but fresh and dizzy, light in their heart.

"Zoey," TJ murmured.

"Yes."

"Is it possible that you might give me another chance?"

"I…" Zoey swallowed. Her eyes darted past him as if she were searching for an escape. Exhaling, she looked at TJ with her wet eyes. "I have a baby now, TJ," she whispered hopelessly. "I don't think you'd be ready to hav—"

TJ silenced her with a kiss. His strong hands cupped her cheeks, and she clenched his shirt, hesitating briefly before wrapping her arms around his neck and kissing him back. It felt awkward at first, but the nerves of her lips recognized the familiar warmness of TJ's. As they shared a breath, Zoey closed her eyes to savor the sweet moment.

CHAPTER 11

The living room in the townhouse wasn't big, and now it was cramped as eight humans, a baby, and a Shiba circled the rectangular coffee table. Balloons, ribbons, garlands, and a golden birthday banner hung on the wall heightened the chaos.

"Hip, hip, hooray!"

"Happy birthday, Zoey!"

"Make a wish!"

Leaning forward, she closed her eyes, whispered her wish, and blew out the candles—shaped like the numbers two and one— before taking in the big smiles of the people surrounding her.

Her twenty-first birthday party had turned out to be very different from what she'd planned. There was no spectacular view of Las Vegas, but it was more wonderful than she had imagined.

She smiled at TJ, who was holding Ella on his lap. The baby giggled when he blew a raspberry on her little palm. He was so different from the spoiled and self-centered boy she'd known. She loved to see them together and was happy that TJ accepted Ella's presence in her life.

Her eyes shifted to Claudia—she hadn't called her *Mom* yet—who was busy talking to Laurel and Nora's mom. Rocket was leaning against her hip, having abandoned Zoey because he didn't like the candle smell.

Claudia was officially living with them and had continued caring for Ella. Like Katya, she also had more friends in the neighborhood than Zoey, and they agreed to babysit Ella or walk Rocket whenever needed. She was touched when Claudia urged her to go back to work or go to grad school.

Nora and Harold's wife were busy talking about quilts at the kitchen counter. For some reason, Zoey's best friend had chosen quilting as her new hobby, and Harold's wife was an expert.

Harold and Jared were watching football on the TV, eating slices of birthday cake. They jumped and shouted whenever their favorite team scored.

"Momma." The voice was soft, but loud enough to silence the adults in the room.

"Did you hear what she said?" Nora rushed in from the kitchen and stood near TJ. The other women followed her.

"I think...*momma*?" TJ looked at Ella.

Claudia pressed her lips, shaking her head. "She is just babbling because she isn't old enough to say any words."

"She's right," Laurel pointed. "Ella is too young to say her first word."

Zoey crouched in front of them when Ella clapped her hands. "What did you say, pumpkin?"

The baby looked at her, showing her toothless smile and stretched her hand, playing with Zoey's hair while babbling the same sound that in her ears resonated like "momma."

"Did you guys hear now?" Zoey scanned around, beaming. "That's 'momma.' Her first word is *momma*."

Lifting her finger, Claudia opened her mouth to contradict, but Laurel's nudge stopped her.

TJ smiled and scooted closer to her. "You know, babe, I believe her first word will be 'momma' because I will train her. Right now, no matter what word she says, you know she loves you as I do." He kissed her cheek and gathered them in his strong arms.

"Ohhh, that's so sweet," Claudia, Laurel, Nora, and her mom exclaimed.

"Your son is such a romantic man," Zoey heard Claudia whisper to Laurel.

"I haven't been surprised because it's running in my family's genes," Laurel answered.

"If you have a single brother, introduce him to me," Claudia teased.

Grinning at their comments, Zoey wrapped the little bundle of joy close to her and leaned herself against TJ's broad shoulder. Her chest was filled with warm and fuzzy feelings like sunshine falling on her face and shoulders under a bright, clear blue sky because everything had fallen into place and now she was where she belonged.

EXCERPT

A WARM RAINY DAY

IN TOKYO

BELLA

"Bella, Bella," The gorgeous stranger whispered.

I let out a quiet sigh because I loved the way he called my name. His voice was gentle, like rustling leaves on a breezy night. With a smile, I tipped my head toward him. The moon hid behind a thin cloud, but its light was enough for me to see his chiseled jaw, long nose, and full, sexy lips.

"I love your baby blue eyes, Bella Bell," he whispered again, lowering his face to mine. "Do you love me?"

"Yes," I whispered back, my heart thundering in my chest as his hazel eyes looked straight at me. *Oh my, he is going to kiss me? Yes ... yes ... Wait, maybe I have to be bolder.* Swallowing, I placed my hands on his muscular hips.

"Bella," he said, caressing my red hair before his hand stopped on the back of my neck and pulled me closer.

I closed my eyes, waiting for his warm kiss to touch mine, but nothing came. Clenching my jaw, I cupped his face with my hands and coaxed it toward me. Oddly, instead of kissing me, he called out, "Bella! Bella! Bella!" At the same moment, I heard loud sounds, like someone banging on the door. *What the …*

As much as I wanted to ignore the annoying interruption, I opened my eyes to find that the handsome, chiseled-jaw guy had disappeared, and my hands clenched my pillow a few inches in front of my face. It wasn't real … but who dared to disturb my dream? I couldn't moan for too long because the banging became louder, followed by my mom's irritated voice. "Bella, how many times do I have to wake you up?"

Ugh, couldn't Mom have woken me up a bit later, at least after I got my kiss? I groaned.

Jumping out of my bed, I opened the door to see my mom glaring at me. She was wearing a blue blazer and pencil skirt, ready for work at a local library as the senior librarian. In her late fifties, she looked great. She had fair skin and no wrinkles, and was a bit heavy at almost five feet tall. Her new hairstyle, short with blonde highlights made her look younger. I could see a flicker of jealousy in my dad's eyes whenever a man glanced at her in awe. How I wished I had inherited her fair skin and would look like her when I was older. However, my older sister got our mom's looks and I looked more like our dad. But thanks to the height from my dad, I was three inches taller than my mom.

A whiff of jasmine from her perfume hit my nose like the fresh air of spring. But my mom's eyes and expression were far from gentle: They were more like a brewing storm.

"Bellalina Elizabeth Bell." Her voice was loud and high when she called my full name—which she did whenever she was super upset. "You aren't a kid anymore. You are almost twenty-two, for God's sake. Why can't you wake up on your own? I can't believe that I have to wake you up like this in the morning," she scoffed, and turned her body toward the kitchen. "Wipe your drool and brush your hair before going out."

The corner of my mouth was damp as I wiped it with the back of my hand. As I followed my mom down to the kitchen, I tied my shoulder-length hair back with the hairband that was always around my wrist.

"That's your fault," I grumbled, and sat on the tall chair at the kitchen island where she'd already put a half gallon of orange juice, a box of cereal, breakfast sausages, six boiled eggs, and a pile of toast, jam, and butter. "I found an effective way to wake up without your help, but you complain about that."

My mom almost rolled her bright blue eyes at me, but she restrained herself. "You set five different alarm clocks to wake you up every day. Five alarms, Bella. You refused to use your phone alarms and bought five metal twin-bell alarm clocks instead. And those are loud enough to wake up the whole neighborhood."

"But that's effective," I protested, helping myself to a glass of orange juice. "You know I'm not a morning person. Then when I found a way that works, you don't like it."

"Those damn alarm clocks can wake up the whole neighborhood," she said slowly as if I didn't comprehend her words the first time. I widened my eyes, and my mom sighed.

She opened her mouth to say something but was interrupted by Mel's entrance. Mel was willowy, five-ten with tan skin and freckles on her nose. She was tying up her long caramel brown hair into a messy topknot.

"Good morning, Mrs. B. Good morning, Bella," Mel chirped.

"Good morning, Mel," my mom and I said in unison.

Mel's full name was Melissa Clinton, and she was twenty-five years old, a first-year graduate student, and our renter. Although her last name was Clinton, she wasn't related to the famous Clintons.

Adele, my older sister by six years, had been Mel's junior high mentor and had always brought Mel to our house. My parents didn't mind, and felt sorry for Mel after learning her parents divorced when she was ten and she lived with her legally blind grandma after that. When her grandma passed away last year, and Adele married and moved to New York, my parents offered Mel my sister's old bedroom, but she insisted on paying rent. Regardless of her position in our house, I always thought of Mel as a sister.

"Another argument about the alarm clocks, I presume?" Mel grinned wider as she sat down next to me. Pouring cereal into an empty bowl, I smiled back at her while my mom finally rolled her eyes.

"Tell her, Mel," Mom said, feigning exhaustion as she picked up her purse and car keys. "She doesn't listen to me."

"I've always listened to you," I complained, my mouth full of cereal.

"Swallow first, then talk," she scoffed, shaking her head. "Okay, girls. I'm leaving now. See you in the evening."

"I'm going to cook for dinner tonight, Mrs. B," said Mel as my mom tapped her shoulder gently and planted a quick kiss on my head.

"No class today?" my mom asked. Her eyes widened as they shifted to Mel.

"Only homework. I have time to cook."

"And what are you going to cook?" she asked with a curious expression. I looked at Mel too.

"Burgers, steamed veggies, and green salad," she answered with confidence, peeling a hard-boiled egg.

I turned away to hide my grin while a smile spread on my mom's lips as she gave an encouraging nod.

Mel was the worst cook. No matter how hard she tried, everything she cooked turned out to be a disaster. The soup was always watery, the pizza was burned, or the grilled chicken was uncooked in the middle. The best meal she could cook was burgers, steamed veggies, and garden salad. No one knew how she never burned the burgers. So, whenever she offered to cook, we could guess her answer.

"Sounds great," my mom said excitedly. "Well, see you tonight, then."

"See ya, Mrs. B," Mel said.

"Bye, Mom," I said as she walked across the living room to the front door. She waved again before closing the door behind her.

"Will you be busy training today?" Mel asked after swallowing her egg. Her hand reached for a second egg and she finished it in three bites before helping herself to two pieces of toast and four breakfast sausages.

Shaking my head, I said, "Not really, but I need to deliver training materials for our new café in San Clemente and introduce myself to the new owner."

"Another new franchise café?" she said, widening her eyes. "It's good to know that Little Bear Café is expanding. Oh, how's about the one in Japan? You mentioned that this summer your company is opening another café there. Is it still happening?"

"Yes, it is. I think the deal should have been closed by now, but I'm not sure," I answered. "We're excited because this will be our second international franchise—after the one in Singapore."

"Ah, I remember when you went to Singapore for a week. So, how many cafes will be opened in Japan?"

I tilted my head, recalling the information. "Bread Lounge – the Japanese company that holds our franchise—will open one in Tokyo, three in Osaka, and more in Kyoto because its headquarters is in the city. The total will be ten. This summer, I'm going to be busy preparing training materials for them. I'm so excited."

Mel nodded, and her green eyes gazed at me from behind her mug. "How about your school? Are you going to continue?"

I groaned silently. When I graduated from high school, I began to work as a data entry clerk at Little Bear headquarters. Because I was a fast learner, my boss suggested to transfer me to the training and development division as an associate instructor to support the café instructors and ensure training sessions run smoothly.

When I got my associate's degree, I was promoted to a café instructor and my days at the office became busier. Then I decided to postpone getting a bachelor's degree. My mom wasn't happy with my decision because she wanted me to get a bachelor's degree and a master's degree like Adele. I wasn't fond of the way my mom always compared me to her, but for the sake of my dad—who was always on my side—I would transfer into the third year of a bachelor's degree student in the fall of this year.

Actually, my mom's demands didn't upset me because my dad understood my decision. For the time being, I was safe from my mom's nagging. What bothered me the most was after Adele left the house, Mel—who used to be my partner in crime—turned into Adele 2.0.

I clearly remembered the last mischievous thing we did. One morning, Mel and I waited for my mom to get her morning juice— we had mixed it with gelatin the night before. It was priceless to see her face when globs of juice dropped into her mug.

But that sweet moment was gone, leaving me with a still-sweet-but-not-fun-anymore Mel.

"Mom should've been happy because I already got my associate's degree. Besides, school and I aren't compatible." I let out a chuckle at my own joke, but Mel didn't smile. I rolled my eyes and continued. "Okay, I'm going to take online school this fall."

"It's going to be tough juggling school and a full-time job," she stated.

"Well," I stood from my seat slowly, unwilling to continue the discussion. "At the moment, my job makes me happy, and my dad seems to agree with me. If my mom doesn't like it, so be it."

Mel watched in dismay as I collected my dirty bowl and glass and brought them to the sink. "Sorry, Bel, I don't mean to make you upset."

Halfway, I stopped and turned to her. "I know you meant well, but don't you know that you sound like Adele now?"

As I spun on my heel, I caught her staring at me incredulously, but I ignored her and left the kitchen after I put the dirty dishes in the dishwasher.

RYO

His computer's clock showed it was almost eleven in the morning, but Ryo Yamada felt as if he'd been in the office forever. Time seemed to run slowly. Was it because of the bad news he'd gotten last night?

Taking a deep breath to release the tightness in his chest, Ryo gazed up at the bright yellow ribbon tied loosely on one of the AC grids waving like a flag. That ribbon reminded him of Akiko, his sister—older by eleven minutes—who loved ribbons and always wore them in her hair.

If he could be honest, he was sick of looking at her with ribbons because there were so many other hair accessories in the world, but she only wore ribbons. However, Ryo had learned not to say anything to make her upset.

His *oneechan* had a congenital heart defect. Their pediatrician had predicted that his sister wouldn't live past three years old, but somehow she survived. When Ryo and Akiko turned seven, the doctor had said she wouldn't live past ten. But his sister was a fighter and was able to live longer than the doctor's predictions. At the age of fifteen, she got a heart transplant that improved her health. Still, her body didn't grow well, and at the age of twenty-five she looked like a sixteen-year-old girl.

Ryo let out a sigh and rolled his sleeves up, revealing his toned arms. He and Akiko were twins, but unlike his sister, he was born healthy. When he was young, each time he asked the question, people around him said he was stronger because he was a boy. He hadn't liked the answer because boys and girls should be the same.

Then one of his uncles explained it to him. Obviously, they shared the same space, but they had different placentas, and somehow there was an imbalance of blood and nutrients flow that favored him and not Akiko. As a result, Ryo grew bigger and stronger while Akiko didn't.

That explanation had haunted him ever since. He had felt responsible for Akiko's condition and kept that thought deep in his mind. The only person who had sensed his guilt was Akiko.

One night, when they were ten, his sister had called him to her room and invited him to sleep next to her. She shared the life and the dreams that she wished to have. Once she finished, she asked Ryo to swear to live the life that she couldn't enjoy. Whatever he did, he would do for them both. Akiko would support him no matter what, even if it meant arguing with their parents.

Ryo agreed and kept his promise as Akiko kept hers.

When Ryo was accepted at UC Berkeley, Akiko was the one who argued with their parents to let him go because it had been her dream to study at that university. She also pushed Ryo to take a job at a prestigious healthcare company in Southern California. Ryo never forgot how brightly her eyes shone when she congratulated him on the new job during their FaceTime.

He owed his oneechan for the life he had in the US.

But all good things must end.

Last night, his mom had called and urged him to return home because Akiko's kidneys were functioning at less than ten percent—a side effect of the immunosuppressant drugs Akiko needed after her heart transplant. His parents thought his presence might give her some emotional support.

The news struck him like lightning. For the hundredth time in his life, Ryo cursed God for only letting his sister live such a short life.

That phone call also put him between a rock and a hard place. He'd gotten his promotion two months ago and wanted to establish his career in his current company. However, Akiko was an important, irreplaceable person in his life. Ryo had sacrificed his dreams for her and would do it again without hesitation. Unfortunately, no matter how much he wished to have the technology to beam him instantly to Tokyo, he couldn't quit on the spot. He was the team leader of an ongoing project in his department, and it would take time to train his replacement. The fastest Ryo could go was next month.

This morning, he submitted his resignation, but his boss refused it and offered him a three-month sabbatical, which was a rare opportunity. Unfortunately, Ryo couldn't guarantee that everything would be back to normal in three months. If something happened to Akiko, it was Ryo's duty to care for his parents, as the only son in the family, which wasn't easy to understand for some people. Heartbroken, he turned down the offer.

His boss was reluctant to let him go, and gave him her personal phone number so Ryo could contact her immediately if a miracle happened and he could return to the States.

Ryo didn't believe in miracles anymore because he'd prayed for years for his sister's health, but still, nothing improved. Would God care enough to listen to his prayers this time?

Letting out another heavy sigh, Ryo unrolled his sleeves and pulled his chair closer to his desk. Tonight, he had to contact Takeru Fujikawa, his best friend, who worked at his parents' real estate company. Takeru could help him find a place to live. Although Ryo could stay in his parents' house, he'd rather have a place for himself. His parents, especially his mom, had dedicated their lives to Akiko. His presence at home would be another burden for his mother. She would be busy cooking for him and wouldn't listen even if he asked her to stop. Ryo preferred to draw a clear line between them. It sounded harsh, but it was for everyone's sake.

"Now it's the tough one," he mumbled as he placed his fingers on the keyboard. They were shaking when he typed "one-way ticket to Tokyo" into Google. It never crossed Ryo's mind that leaving this country would be difficult for him. He stopped and scrubbed a hand over his face.

"Don't be selfish. This is for oneechan," he hissed, clenching his jaw.

The scolding worked.

Ryo's mind calmed, and his fingers stopped shaking. In less than twenty minutes, he found an affordable airline ticket.

(find out more...)

ACKNOWLEDGEMENT

At the end of 2021, I wrote this novella with a thought to post it as a series in Kindle Vella and had planned to publish my fourth romance novel set on Bali Island in the summer of 2023. However, because of many challenges over the past year, I decided to change my plan. Instead, I rewrote Zoey's story and turned it into a novella under the genre of Women's fiction with a touch of mystery and romance.

Unlike my previous three novels that were light-hearted stories written from a mix of points of view, this novella is more emotional and melancholic. Also, it is written from third-person point of view. It was a challenge, but I found that I enjoyed it more than I expected, and at a certain level, it even felt more straightforward than first-person point of view.

Now please allow me to extend my gratitude to people who have been on my journey and bringing this story to see the world.

Thanks to The Pro Book Editor for giving feedback, editing, and proofreading this story.

Thanks to my dear husband, Steve, for your endless love and encouragement.

Thanks to my family and close friends for moral support.

Special thanks to Icha for allowing me to use her baby girl's name in this novel. Ella is a beautiful name, indeed.

Thanks to Joy and her husband for helping me find a perfect Chinese name for one of the characters in this novella.

Thanks to God for blessing me with a talent to write, enabling me to create this book and, of course, more in the future.

Lastly, thanks to all readers for taking the time to read this novella. Your support in my work means a lot to me. I hope you don't mind telling your friends and family about this novella and writing a short review at your favorite online retailer's website.

Happy reading.

ABOUT THE AUTHOR

KANA WU is a bilingual author who writes her novels in English as her second language. She also enjoys traveling and incorporates the places she visits into her books.

Her debut novel, *No Romance Allowed*, won the Romance category for the 2020 TCK Publishing Readers' Choice Awards Contest.

Her second novel, *No Secrets Allowed*, earned a 1st Place Blue Ribbon for the Chatelaine Book Awards for Romantic Fiction, a division of the 2021 Chanticleer International Book Awards.

Currently, she resides in beautiful Southern California with her husband, surrounded by her books and the occasional hummingbird or wild bird visitors.

Keep up with Kana's latest news and updates by visiting her website or following her on social media.

 https://www.facebook.com/kanawuauthor
 https://www.instagram.com/kanawuauthor
 www.kanawuauthor.com

Made in the USA
Coppell, TX
14 June 2023